T0082889

Learning Long Words

WILLIAM GAILLARD ELLIS JR

authorHOUSE®

AuthorHouse™
1663 Liberty Drive
Bloomington, IN 47403
www.authorhouse.com
Phone: 833-262-8899

© *2021 William Gaillard Ellis Jr. All rights reserved.*

No part of this book may be reproduced, stored in a retrieval system, or transmitted by any means without the written permission of the author.

Published by AuthorHouse   07/01/2021

ISBN: 978-1-6655-3089-7 (sc)
ISBN: 978-1-6655-3090-3 (e)

Print information available on the last page.

Any people depicted in stock imagery provided by Getty Images are models, and such images are being used for illustrative purposes only.
Certain stock imagery © Getty Images.

This book is printed on acid-free paper.

Because of the dynamic nature of the Internet, any web addresses or links contained in this book may have changed since publication and may no longer be valid. The views expressed in this work are solely those of the author and do not necessarily reflect the views of the publisher, and the publisher hereby disclaims any responsibility for them.

Chapter 1

JOEY WALKED DOWN WEST UNIVERSITY'S HALLWAY NOT REALLY wanting to be a sub teacher for the sixth grade English class. It was the farthest from his mind when he was called they needed a sub and now he'll be subbing for six classes a day for two weeks. That would mean he would have to actually teach instead of setting before a class handing out a pop quiz.

If he didn't need the money he would have said, "No way. But two weeks pay beats a day now and then any day. But starting on a Friday will give the children a change to think over what he was planning.

"Just hope I don't get in trouble," he thought as he walked into his first class.

The room became quiet as he sat his case on the desk given them a smile as he pulled out his Roster Sheets, a stack of hand outs, paper and pens.

Then turning to the black board he picked up the caulk and wrote, "My name is Mr. Joey Holgominerykamo."

He wanted to laugh seeing the shock on their faces upon seeing his last name and hearing several girls trying to pronounce it.

When he was again before his desk, he calmly said, "Rather you just call me Mr. Joey."

After rearranging the papers, he Looked up and across the class a second then using his best command voice said, "I will be your teacher for the next two weeks and I will do the best I can to make sure you learn something. Now first I need a head count."

Thought a second before he pointed to the girl in green pants and brown top ask, "How would you like to be my head counter?"

The dark brown headed girl pointed to herself having a surprise look on her face as she answered saying, "Me."

Joey held out the roster sheet with a pen attached saying, "Are you not the prettiest Brown Hair girl in school." His words brought laughter and a few "Yes's and No's and he could see the girl was blushing.

So holding up his hands and walking around desk to face the class he said, "Hold on now. There more to this then what you think. For the next two weeks, the person that takes the head count will be prettiest girl or the handsomest boy in this class room for a day and will get an extra A grade if they bring to me in the next 2 weeks a short story that is not over two pages long of what it feels like to be the ugliest girl or boy in school."

Laughter broke out as his meaning became clear.

Then Joey look back at the Brown headed Girl and said, "Would like to be first to take up my challenge?"

The girl looks at Mr. Joey and the way he expressed himself to her made her fill happy as she answered saying, "Sure, I'll take up your challenge and be the prettiest brown haired girl in this class room for a day."

Joey who gave her a smile before he waved an open hand at her saying, "For today we have the prettiest Brown Hair Girl in this class room and I want everyone here to treat her as such all day long. I want you to go around bragging on her beautiful looks. I want you give her a vision of what it like to be the prettiest girl in her English Class for one day and maybe tomorrow she will bring me a short story one or two pages of what it would be like being the ugliest brown hair girl in school."

Laughter exploded across the room with the added jabber among them and became quiet as she took the roster and as she did, Joey stepped back and clapped quickly followed by the other children.

As the children calmed down with only couple friends joking with her, Joey turned back to his desk, he asking, "Will couple of you guys please pass out the dictionaries and class as they do, please clear your desk of any writing material."

By the time he took his seat overlooking the children three boys had already passed out the Dictionaries and as they took their seat Joey said, "You are all wondering what this crazy teacher is up to now. It is written all over your young faces. For the next two weeks we are going to have a long word contest."

Joey stood and walking toward the door thinking "Where are they" when suddenly through the door came a big giant TV Screen and a long table on wheels with six Word Writer units mounted on it and six chairs. The two guys slowly pushing the stuff in said, "We been waiting outside and didn't want to disturb the class while you were introducing yourself to the kids."

"Thanks," is all Joey answered.

It took them just a second to have everything in good operation condition and Joey thanked them as they left. Then turning to the class, Joey could see the children had what the hack written all over their faces.

He wanted to laugh as he pointed to the word writers then pointing toward the screen saying, "This TV Screen we have here will display the many words you will write using these word writers on the table. Let me show you an example and you can understand clearer."

Joey call up a four letter display and there before the children was screen full of four letter words in rows one space apart and no commas. The children became mumbling when one of the girls said, "We are to fine 4 letter words in the dictionary and write the word we fine on the word writer?"

"No, no," Joey answered as he clear the screen before he looked across the class room faces giving them a big smile as he tried to present his words with a little sneaky sound to it with a body movement to help said, "Far bigger words than 4 letter words you will be looking up."

Walking around the table he pointed to the word writers saying, "There is a catch to this process. When you find a word, let's say we are doing a ten letter word, you cannot bring the dictionary with you to write the word, you must do it from memory and if you misspell the word you must leave the Writer and fetched the correct spelling. The writer will give you 15 seconds to correct and you punish your class mates by holding up the line so make sure you spell it correctly the first time."

Joey smiled giving them his most wicked looked and as he turned back to his desk even gave them an old evil laugh while rubbing his hands which brought the classroom echoing with laughter.

Still rubbing his hands he said, "You see for anyone to be able write a word on the writer they must enter their seat number."

He then leans back and lowered his head as he pointed to the writers before saying, "We have six writers and we have six rows of desks and we have eight desks in each row. So who can tell me what their number would be to be able to write on the Word Writer?"

When no answer came Joey point to the row by the door saying, "I give you a hint. This row by the door is the "A" row."

Then pointing to the next said, "B row."

Still no answer so he pointed to the C Row saying, "The first seat in this row of desks is C1 and the neck seat is C2 and," the C3 he did not get too for the girl sitting in C3 seat said, "My number would be C3."

Quickly the children caught onto what was to be their number and the rumbling quieted Mr. Joey sat down at his desk said, "For the first day, I'll go easy on you and not require you seeking ten letter words. But to start this game, I will only have you seeking out seven letter words. I have six classes today and in each class they will also be doing the same thing and the class that can place the most words on the screen or fill it up will get a reward. What that will be has yet to be determined for I must go by school rules."

Mr. Joey left his seat and as he stood beside the Word Writers he said, "Today we will begin with only 7 letter words and I almost forgot I want all paper and pens off the desk with only the dictionaries remaining."

There was a few morning and complaining as they put their papers away and Mr. Joey could see some of the girls already had several words written down.

As their desks cleared Mr. Joey said, "It is now 8:20 so when the clock reaches 8:30 we will begin and I will stop you at 8:50 given the class 20 minutes to fill up the screen with as many seven letter words they can find. We have six rows of desks and as you can see there are six Word Writers. Each desk row has a Word Writer and I believe you can understand why each Word Writer has a letter beside it. It means that is your row writer if one writer has no one writing on it you cannot use it to write your seven letter word on it. The Writer will not OK your seat number. Remember you have only 15 seconds to spell the word right and 15 seconds to check the definition and the whole class has only 20 minutes to try to fill the screen. You can only write one word down at a time and you must leave and let your team mate place their word next. For you are in a contest, children between your class and other five English classes and they also will only have twenty minutes to see how many seven letter words they can place on the screen. There will be no talking or helping another spell a word and if you misspell a word you cannot change it for another word until you have corrected the word you were trying to write in the first place. Remember if you fail walk back to your desk and find out what you did wrong. There will be no talking, pushing, or rushing."

But as he returned back to his desk he knew those words went in one ear and out the other but looking back across the class room it did appear most of the children caught onto the game.

He took a deep breath as the clock neared the start time thinking, "Hope this works."

As the room became quiet, he let the clock do the talking as he watched the children and could see some were still searching the dictionary but most seem to have their 7 letter word ready to record and did he ever want to laugh as soon for as the clock bang out 8:30 the children left their seats rushing to place their word in the system. Some had it right some had it wrong. Some had the word but forgot what it meant but slowly the screen began to fill with 7 letter words but still was only a little over halfway filled when the time ran out.

As the children morn regaining their seating, Mr. Joey stood saying, "Well done children and I want you to give this English Class a name using a word that is not over 20 letters and not less than 14 letters. After all you are in a contest and I think you should have a name worthy of being call Class #1 don't you think?"

There was many agreeing with him around the room before Mr. Joey said, "You have until the contest is over or I will continue to call you, "Class #1."

Suddenly the bell to end the class rung out and had the same boys collect the Dictionaries, Mr. Joey dismisses the Class calling out, "Good luck."

As the last child left Joey cleared the screen to prepare for the next class before he leaned back in the chair, giving himself a pat on the back thinking, "That went way better than I thought it would. I never would imagine they would have found sixty-three 7 letter words in twenty minutes, but they did."

Joey glance as the first child who had entered for the next class Joey thought, "I wonder how many words they will fine next week when I make them find large words having the same meaning as a smaller letter word."

As the room slowly filled with new faces, Joey stood to face them thinking, "When my two weeks are over, I bet they never ask me to sub again."

When it seems the last child to sit had entered, Joey wrote his name across blackboard saying, "As you can see my last name is hard to pronounce so call me, "Mr. Joey."

Chapter 2

MR. JOEY THANKED THE LAST TWO BOYS LEAVING FOR COLLECTING the dictionaries and on one of the empty Black Board began to draw out a record with the words across the top saying seven, then eight, then 9 and continued till he had 20 and across the top wrote number of Letters in each word. Then as he was just finishing placing the class lines crossing the vertical line when some young and very attractive women stuck her head into the room saying, "You sure have gotten the children a talking I do say."

As he made sure the score board was neat as he could before he answered her saying, "My Dad had this system setup for sighing in over at his work place and they upgraded and I modified the system to use in this word game that I came up to challenge the kids. So far the last three classes seem to have gone bunkers over it so far."

All the while he was talking he was able to walk around his desk and as he got close he held out his hand saying, "My name is Joey Williams and my I ask are you subbing as I am for two weeks?"

But she took a stepped back with a pretty smile said, "But from what I heard from the children, your last name was so unpronounceable they had to use your first name and call you Mr. Joey."

"Just a trick for them to remember my name," Joey answer before asking, "You know my name, what's yours?"

She gave him a smile while rubbing her face thinking should he tell him or not when some kid walking by said, "Her name is Gracie Shoemaker, she twenty-two and she single."

"Charlie," she hollered at him for after he had spoken, Charlie took off running with Gracie calling after him saying, "You better run. Wait till I get hold of you when we get home."

As she turned back to face Joey, to him the outline of her face was quite beautiful as she said, "That was, Charlie my baby brother. We were supposed to have lunch together."

Not passing up the opportunity to know this beauty girl more Joey asked, "Mind if I join you and Charlie for lunch."

"I don't see why not," Gracie answered as she waved for him to follow her and as Joey left the room only to be met by Charlie who asked, "Mr. Joey you single also."

"Yes," Joey answer as they began to walked down the empty hall way where off in the distance they could just hear the school's cafeteria buzzing with the six grade student's gibberish but at the end of the hallway Gracie turned left saying, "Subs and teachers eat this way."

Before he could ask her what was the food like when Gracie left him and began walking real fast leaving Joey to answer another of Charlie's questions who asked, "How old are you Mr. Joey?"

"Twenty-three," he answered given up trying to keep up with Gracie and walked along with Charlie asking "What is her rush?"

Charlie almost laughing answered, "She was supposed to meet some boyfriend today for lunch and I guess she just remember he was coming."

"In that case I better enter the Teacher's Lounge with her," Joey answered as he sprinted to catch up with her.

As he settled beside her which caused her to slow down and glancing upon Joey she notices in the brighter lighting he had a strong looking body and handsome face and there was a charm about him she never encountered before causing her to be an instant friend with him and this frustrated her for there was a little more attraction then she was expecting as she gave a glance upon his groin area before slowing to an even slower pace saying, "I probably to late already. My first date in three months and I'm late and he probably heard rumors about me and would have ditched me before we got to know each other."

Then turning to Joey, she hit him on the arm saying, "I'm late and it's your fault."

Joey, while rubbing his arm, gave Gracie his best smile saying, "Then why not let me be your date instead?"

Gracie stopped and was a little shocked at Joey's boldness and giving him her best sexy look said, "Before that can happen you must first asked me out don't you think."

"I do," Joey given a shocked answer before giving her a glance from her toes to her hair and making sure his face was serious he turns toward Charlie and waving for him to come closer and then led Charlie closer to the lockers and kneeing down asked, "Is she dangerous?"

But Charlie while almost laughing whisper back, "She just looking for a sucker and I think it is you."

"But Charlie she so beautiful," Joey asked but Charlie returned a, "That may be true but Daddy calls her "Crazy Gracie" and every date she went on after the first date the guy was never seen again. I heard they even left the state to stay clear of her."

His words only brought both to laughter and when Charlie glanced back at Gracie he notice she had her hands behind her back while swishing her toe in and out as she turn herself around in some dance mood.

Glancing back at Charlie he smile saying, "Crazy or not, I'm dating her."

He left Charlie's laughter and as he a got upped, he got close to Gracie, almost touching her, he asked, "Would you like to go dancing at the six and seven grade dance here at the school tonight?"

She leaned forward and still with hands behind her back stopped her dancing and looking Joey hard in his hazel eyes before she left him walking toward the Teachers' lounge and calmly said, "I taught you would never ask but isn't that where there is drinking and nasty old men always wanting to dance with us sweet beautiful girls."

Charlie was still laughing as Joey caught onto Gracie's joking answered with, "Oh no, it is not like that at all. The people own the place and it's full of good looking guys and girls."

As they were about to enter the Cafeteria, they had to stopped, for several teachers were leaving and each gave them a glance as Gracie said, "My mother told me to stay away from this School Dances because it was full of bad dancers and could cause me to gain bad habits."

Suddenly Charlie broke their discussion saying, "We better eat. Forth Period Class starts in ten minutes."

An older teacher let them enter cafeteria and as they passed her, she said "Two love birds if I ever saw one" and as she left the room added, "Heard about your contest Joey, great idea. It does have the children talking."

Joey looked at the older teacher and gave her a smile which only made the old teacher laugh as she left the area. But Gracie paid her no mind as she was pointing out to the waiter what she wanted, two orders of tenders and fires.

Charlie, now beside her as she said, "I want Honey Mustard."

Joey just order of couple of the fried cheese sticks and by the time he got them, Gracie and Charlie had done gobbled their food down.

"Hungry were we," Joey asked as follow them out the door finishing off the last fried cheese and chicken stick.

As they entered the hallway, they were quickly walking among the children heading for their class when in the middle of the hallway trying to say it over the noised of the children Gracie turned to Joey saying, "I'll was going with Charlie to the dance anyway so why don't we meet here in the Gym tonight and let me see how good a dancer you are."

Her words brought silence to the children around them who were now watching them curious to what Joey's answer will be who did not hesitate by answering, "I'll meet you here and I'll show you." There were a few giggles and as the children separated allowing him to continue toward his room glancing back just catching Gracie entering her class room with several of the children asking her about him.

Most of the children were already seated with several examining the Word Writer as he enters and just as he took his seat, Professor Jinn stuck his head in the door and with an added finger effect said, "Joey, I need to talk to you."

Now Joey has known Professor Jinn all his life for he was their next door neighbor. But when he was a kid he called them Mr. and Mrs. Jinn. He kept a well-trimmed yard and when he was out looking for lawns to mow to make a buck or two, Mr. Jinn never did let him mow his yard and fuss if he got caught running around in it. But Mrs. Jinn was a sweetheart and many times he went home with a box full of sweets she had made always saying, "We can't ever eat this many cookies or this many sweet rolls." But never was a cake and when he asked her why, her answer was simple a "Waste of time and money and always ends up in the trash."

Quickly he left his desk and as he walked out into the hallway only to hear Mr. Jinn say, "Joey, as Assistance Principle I was supposed to be informed ahead of time about any special event someone was going to have in their class rooms. But from the reactions the school children are having over this contest between English Classes has a good ring to it so I'm letting you continue."

Before Joey could say anything, Mr. Jinn left him waving his hand saying, "Your class is waiting."

"Well," Joey was thinking as he entered to fine several of the children scrambling back for their seats. He just stood by the door glancing over the class and their concern faces and smile as he said, "You should know by now my name is Mr. Joey."

Chapter 3

CHARLIE SET HIS BOOKS IN HIS LOCKER AND AS HE FOLLOWED BILL toward their last class, Mr. Joey's English class and as he was stepping away from his locker into the Hallway, he just missed running into Maryann who just said, "Watch were you're going Charlie and we better hurry are we'll be late for Mr. Joey's class."

Charlie yelled back, "Its Mrs. Watson's Class."

But Maryann stopped and turning to face Charlie said, "It was Mrs. Watson English but it is now, Mr. Joey's Class and from the stories I've heard about this contest between classes I think it is going to be fun and I bet our Class can win. So come on guys lets rumble."

Both Charlie and Bill gave her a "Go get it" laughed for Maryann has been and always will be the cheerleader and cheering everyone on to make an "A" on a test ever since Bill and Joey first met her in first grade. Cheering in races they played at and would let both Bill and him jump rope without screaming at them to leave, go play with the boys, or singing out "Girls only."

They like to jump rope and would do it as often as they could whenever Maryann and her friend Sandra were swinging the rope or they beg her or Sandra to swing it for them which they did yelling at them in their play.

Sandra was just like Maryann in many ways and during dance classes on Friday afternoon would either be Bill's or Charlie's dance partner and Maryann seemed in the long run always end up dancing with Charlie. He liked to dance with her and dating girls had been wondering around in his mind lately and a thought hit him as he followed Maryann as she carried her books next to her with several papers sticking out of her books corners he asked, "Maryann, Gracie got a hot date tonight over at Linda's Dance Club and Bill and I are going. You want to come with us and we'll dance every song."

His words stopped Maryann in her tracks and turning herself to face Charlie asked, "Only if Sandra can come also."

Bill realizing what Charlie was asking butted in saying, "Sandra must come along for sure."

Maryann waved her hands laughing saying, "We already know about the dance and Gracie has already invited us."

As Charlie and Bill followed her into the Class room, they were whispering about who they were going to dance with but stopped for as soon as Maryann entered, she sang out, "We are the sixth and last English class and we are going to win this contest."

But Mr. Joey corrected her saying, "Class, there is no contest today it starts Monday and will last for two weeks."

Then turning to Charlie with a little authority sound to it said, "You three are late so why don't you three pass out the dictionaries as punishment and collect them at the end of class."

Only Bill answered saying "Yes sir" as they quickly obeyed him.

As Charlie took his seat at his desk located behind Bill's asked, "Bill, did you get a good look at these dictionaries we just passed out."

Bill turned his very boyish face slightly toward Charlie and whispered back, "I sure did and they sure have been used and abused today for sure." His words only cause them and the others around them to break into hysterical laughter causing Maryann to hooch at them.

Charlie fingered his dictionary as Mr. Joey describe the equipment and what it does and when Mr. Joey brought up the screen full of words only having four letters, it pert Charlie's interest and a clearer understanding of the challenge the whole class had before them became apparent remembering Maryann words, "We are in a contest and our class can win."

Mr. Joey brought his attention back to the class saying, "I need one person to take the head count."

Only silence greeted him so with an evil looking smile he pointing at Charlie saying, "Charlie, how would you like to do the headcount for today."

Than with a begging motion, he said, "And also become one of the handsomest boys in school for a day and tonight when you go dancing tonight you will be known as the handsomest boy on the dance floor."

Laughter broke out in the class as Charlie now wearing a big smile stood to get the roster bowed to the class several times while saying, "Sure."

MaryAnn hooch the class several more times as Mr. Joey handed Charlie the list saying, "Before the end of the contest two weeks from now you will right me a two-page short story what it is like to be the ugliness boy in school, understand Charlie?"

Then turning to the class said, "As I have told the other classes, anyone of you, if you want, can also write me a two-pages short story on anything for extra credit."

Turning back to Charlie he notices he this questionable look on his face as Charlie asked, "You want me to write a two-page story on what it is like to be the ugliness boy in school because today I am the handsomest boy in school if I do the headcount?"

"That is about right," Mr. Joey answered.

"What if I don't take the job," Charlie then asked having a slight smile, thinking, "Got him now."

But Mr. Joey countered with, "I'll just ask another is all."

"Yes, I'll do it," Charlie quickly answered meekly already wondering what he would write as he turned to the list of students and as he did, Mr. Joey said, "Every class I will require someone to do the roster and become the handsomest boy in school for a day or the prettiest girl in school but you must give me a two-page short story what it is like to be the ugliness girl or boy in school. Now what girl would like to be the prettiest girl in school for Monday's class?"

Mr. Joey was wondering did he have to appoint a girl when MaryAnn spoke up saying. "I will."

"Good, and Monday I want the class to honor all the Queens for a day for these boys and girls may never become great beauties but for one day in the sixth grade they will be."

Suddenly MaryAnn asked, "Can we wear what we want."

Mr. Joey looked at Charlie a second thinking before turning to MaryAnn for her question had not popped in his mine so he said, "I haven't been asked that question but I guess it will be ok as long as it represents you and makes you as beautiful as you are now."

Then turning back to the game, he pointed toward the clock saying, "In five minutes you will start putting in words with only seven letters long. Prepare yourselves."

Again Mr. Joey let the clock do the talking thinking, "Maryann just may make this Class a winner. She sure got the bossy way about her."

By now Charlie and Bill along with the others around them were beginning to search the dictionary for words having only seven letters and he quickly found the word "Balance" just as the clock struck 2:30 and as everybody was getting up to enter their word, Maryann yelled "Stop, seat number one first followed by number two, then three and so on. I will have order and I say let's win this contest."

A loud "Yea" came back to her as they began to take a seat to enter their word but as they were finishing, Mary Ann again called out, "Remove the chairs, seating takes ten to thirty seconds of our time."

Charlie quickly followed Fred entering his first word "Balance," answered the question and was entering his seventh word "Disease" when their time ran out.

He returned to his seat as Mr. Joey called out saying, "Today was not a contest but to let you gain experience in entering your words and for you to know the rules of the game. You have done as great as the other classes and may just be the winner, never know. First thing, I want you to choose a name for your class besides being called Class #6. I want the name to be not over 20 letters in it and not less than 14 and if you don't, I will just call you Class #6 and I hope you all have a nice weekend."

Bill was already placing his homework books in his bike's basket and was pulling out his bicycle from the bike rack when Charlie arrived and as he was doing the same asked, "You know we have our first game tomorrow and I'm hoping Couch Tomas picks me to pitch tomorrow."

"Never know about him and his bright ideas," Charlie returned which cause them to bust out in laughter as they began to walk their bikes toward the Schoolyard's exit.

"I think Maryann made us late again," Bill asked as did several fake moves as if he was getting on his bike.

Charlie understanding Bill words as he said, "I wish I could ride my bike or at lease run to the exit with it and you know we can't do that."

Bill looked over at Charlie and almost laughed as he said, "Especially what will happen after Mrs. Nosy body across the street calls the Principle and nobody wants to be caught by her and her big mouth. I know one thing you can't talk yourself out having to place your bike out on the street."

Both broke out in laughter.

As Charlie calmed down he said "And poor Milton, had to leave his bike out on the street for a week or more."

"That was because he called Mrs. Nosy a "Nosy Bitch." Bill answered and his words only brought on more laughter.

As they settle down and neared the exit Bill began swinging his right arm as if he was throwing a pitch saying, "I hope Couch Tomas picks me to pitch tomorrow. I bet I've thrown a thousand stripes since we started baseball practice. I never did hit the dummy Couch Thomas place in the Batter's box."

"Not me, I bet I hit that dam thing twenty times or more," Charlie answered before saying sadly, "All I threw was balls and I may get a strike now and then."

Bill returned a, "I think I threw the same way, but I threw all strikes and no balls."

He then gave Charlie a sideways glance and with a smile saying, "Really."

They both were laughing as they climbed upon their bikes and as they settled Charlie answered saying, "I don't want to be a pitcher myself. I want to be the third basemen. He gets all the action."

Bill began to pedal home cried back, "I thought the catcher was what you wanted and it was where all the action was," Charlie yelled back "I never said that and I'll see you at the dance and where pink."

Bill did not return an answer as he got off his bike having to cross the street at the flags and he could see Mrs. Nosy nose at the window for when you see that nose print on the window, you know Mrs. Nosy is watching and that when he notices Sandra was one of the flaggers at the other crossing and he knew that she only did it whenever one of the normal flaggers were sick.

So dodging the other children he quickly pushed his bike toward the crossing and as he followed the other kids across he was trying to finds the words to say to her but as he came to Sandra holding her flag down stopping the traffic, Bill stopped before her saying, "Hello Sandra and you look great in your flag girl outfit. Where's Frank anyway."

"Grandma died and they had her funeral today," she answered before shaking the flag in a motion for him to move on while saying, "Move along Bill, I've getting tired of holding the fag and I'll see you at the dance tonight."

"Not if I don't see you first," Bill hollered back as he began to peddle his bike for home.

Now Charlie on the other hand, after leaving the school ground did not get far, for as he turned on Amherst toward home there awaited Maryann saying, "Charlie, we need to work out a plan for Mr. Joey's contest. I want our class to win."

"Don't see how you can improve on what we have already done," he returned while getting off his bike to walk with her.

"There must be more we can do," she then asked.

But before he could answer her Mother pull up hollering," Stop flirting with Charlie and get in or we'll be late to get our hair done for the dance tonight." "Yes, Mother," she returned and as she got into the passenger seat very serious said, "Charlie, please think about what I asked, please."

Charlie watched them leave a second before climbing back on his bike to ride toward the house and as he settles down peddling at his cruising speed, he began to think about the two-page short story he had to write, "I bet he wants me to use big words. Twenty letters long at lease. But what am I going to say on those two pages telling what it is like to be the ugliness boy in school."

"I could say I look like a pig," he said with a little laughter and as he parked his bike in the garage, picked upped his homework and turned toward the kitchen whispered, "At lease I have two weeks to come up with something."

Chapter 4

CHARLIE STOPPED AS HE ENTERED THE JR HIGH GYM AND TO HIS right he quickly notices Mr. Joey talking to Mrs. Sonamaker their Principle under the basketball net. The sound system was set up behind her and he knew that she who will not let anybody near the sound system and watched Mr. Joey hand her several records and CDs. Glanced over at the girls' bleachers, he just catches his sister being hug by Maryann who was dressed in a light blue blouse and skirt that reached the floor given her teenage face the image of beauty.

Suddenly he was lightly pushed from behind by Bill who said, "Get in there Charlie. They want let you dance out here."

Turning as he caught himself, Charlie answered with, "Hello Bill, just looking to what I gotten myself into and Maryann and Sandra is already here," then pointing, "See, their sitting over there with Gracie in the girl's section."

"You going to dance with your sister aren't you," Bill asked as he headed for the Boys side of the bleachers. But Charlie did not answer as he followed noticing there was way more girls than boys but thought "It still early."

As they neared the bleachers, Frank called out, "Charlie, you going to be dancing with Maryann all night?"

"Yea," George added before saying, "And Bill, are you going to be dancing with Sandra all night? We want to dance with them at least once."

His words brought laughter among the boys with a few more saying, "I want to dance with them also."

Charlie just shook his head "no" before pointing toward the girls saying, "There is way more girls then us so I plain on dancing with every one of them."

Then from behind him came Mr. Joey's Voice saying, "I think Charlie is right you should try to dance with every girl. After all, isn't that what you came here to do? Have fun."

Turning, Charlie found Mr. Joey walking toward the restroom which was just past their bleachers and said, "That was what I was thinking."

Mr. Joey stopped and gave Charlie a smile saying, "But I heard Maryann and Sandra say they were only going to dance with Charlie or Bill."

Hearing only silence, he turned back toward the Restroom to wash up and comb his darn curly hair thinking, "This is going be fun to watch."

Charlie and Bill followed with the silence being broken by George calling out, "Run chickens and you can't hide Maryann and Sandra will find you." His words brought laughter among the boys with a few agreeing."

Then as they followed Mr. Joey into the Restroom Charlie asked, "Mr. Joey can you help us. We don't want to dance with Maryann and Sandra all the time. What can we do?"

But Mr. Joey asked, "Is your sister a good dancer."

The question caught Charlie by surprise stopping his begging. Looked at Bill then he looked back at Mr. Joey, who was now washing his hands before answering saying, "Is she good. She is the best and she been on many dancing dates just to go dancing. Couples are always stopping or calling to get her to go dancing with them."

Bill added, "She started to teach me how to dance when I first met Charlie in kindergarten. Our moms are sisters so when I spent the night with Charlie, Gracie would get us to dance with her."

"She sure did," Charlie said before adding, "And when Bill was not around, she still got me to dance with her and it was fun and now I and Bill are the best dancers in school and if we are not careful the girls will be fighting over us like the last dance."

"And what you do last dance that caused the girls to cry over you," Mr. Joey asked thinking as he wiped his hands dry, "This ought to be good."

Charlie looked at Bill who pointed his fingered at him and whispered, "You tell it."

Turning back to Mr. Joey, Charlie wanted to laugh as he said, "Well last dance Maryann and Sandra were sick and could not come so we were free to dance with anyone."

Suddenly Bill started to laugh causing Charlie to join him after he said, "Mr. Joey, when we went to let one girl off and asked who would like to dance with us sometimes you should have seen them fight to get to us first. The girls even go out on the dance floor and tap the girl I was dancing with on the shoulder and ask would she mine letting let her butt in."

Still creaking up Bill said, "Charlie's right and he is telling you the truth and I bet right now their already fighting to see who is first. I saw Susan and Linda pointing at us when we came in."

Charlie more settled asked, "Mr. Joey, what are we to do?"

Joey look at these young men understanding really how funny is was to get themselves in such a situation. That was one thing he never had to worry about so he said, "Now boys, I do agree it is funny to be wanted in such away. Now if you were me, you are here to dance and I got my eyes on one girl but I will let the others have a piece me now and then letting my number one girl rest. For girls can do a lot of things but only a few can out last the boys when it comes to dancing."

Joey left them and as he enters the gym he heard Charlie say, "Let's do as he said and my number one girl is Maryann."

He was laughing as he crosses the gym floor toward his seat with the other teachers and glancing over at the girl's section Joey could still Gracie sitting with Maryann and Sandra but her eyes were upon him so he gave her a little wave, a smile and did a waltz moved and almost bumped into Mr. Jinn who said "Careful Joey" and as he walk pass Joey toward Mrs. Shoemaker added, "Better fine a seat, the dance about to start."

"Yes Mam," Joey answered, gave a glance at Gracie and notice her and the other girls were smiling watching him.

Changing directions, he walks toward them and as he near the girl section, he gave Gracie his best smile asking, "May I have the first dance with you."

Gracie stood and walking toward him said, "I thought you never asked." Then grabbing his arm, she leads Joey out onto the dance floor saying, "This is my first dance so I guess you can be my partner."

Joey let her lead him as they came to rest in the middle of the Gym, Mr. Jinn standing before the mike said, "Is everybody ready to dance?"

The gym erupted with the children given back their answer as they settled down he said, "But for the first dance of the night will be done by your teachers."

There was some discussing among the teachers but all remain seated leaving only Joey and Gracie on the dance floor and Mr. Jinn said, "It's a waltz."

At Mr. Jinn's words, Joey stepped in front of Gracie saying, "I love to waltz how about you?"

"That I do," She answered as she settled into Joey's arms to dance wondering maybe Joey does know how to dance and him willing dance before everyone surprised her.

Slowly all the lights were turned off around the edge of dance floor and as the lights dimmed above them, as soon as Mrs. Shoemaker started the Tennessee Waltz, Joey and Gracie stepped forth into the music with Gracie following Joey's lead.

In perfect timing they began waltzing to the music with Joey allowing Gracie to show off with her beautiful spins. She was easy to dance with and was he ever enjoying it as he looked down into her eyes as their bodies touched. As one they cross the dance floor each forgetting all forgot all about the children or those watching. It was their joy of dancing that overcame them, the movement of their bodies as they flowed with the music together. The sweet change of hand movement as Gracie spun herself around in his arms. The strength in them allowed her to show off while Joey calmly waltzed into her spin. The Gracie in her matched her name each time Joey spin her, showing off, feeling the smoothness of her skin, the sweet smell of her perfume she wore and her eyes seeming to be always upon him as they waltz.

He had forgotten what it was having great dancer in his arms. It felt wonderful being the first dance he been too since High school. He was just like these kids for he went to school here also and glancing over at the other teachers realizing most knew him and his dancing skills and must know hers is why there still sitting watching them dance. But as the song ended Gracie and Joey took several more turns and was Joey ever smiling as they finish allowing Gracie to do one more spin.

The children exploded with shouting and clapping as Joey calmly took a step away and gave Gracie a bow and looked at the children raising his arm toward her saying, "Isn't she the greatest."

Her answer was several bows to the clapping.

Suddenly Mr. Jinn called out "Let's dance and its girls choice turn" just as Mrs. Shoemaker started one of Joey's records, a nice get to know ya two step began to Echo across the Gym flood.

Calmly Gracie moved into Joey's waiting arms asking, "Would you like to dance."

Joey calmly said "I thought you would never ask" as he calmly led her into the music as children began to dance quietly around them.

As they moved to the music Gracie asked, "Rumors about you are true. You can dance."

Joey could only looked into her blue eyes as he slowly began to led her into the two step circle saying, "I guess it just comes naturally,"

But Gracie countered asking, "Then how come your not married with your naturally abilities?"

"Never met one that I wanted to live with all my life," Joey answered as he led her into a dance move allowing her make a nice dance spin hoping to get her mind off of him.

But it was not to be as she came back into his arms Gracie asked, "What you been doing besides substitute teaching." Then she fluttered her eyes at him with a smile.

He wanted to laugh at her actions as they became more relaxed dancing together and before he could answer her the music stopped. As they separated Joey held onto Gracie's hand and silently the two stood together watching the children separate and he could see Charlie and Maryann still on the dance floor together as was Bill and Sandra and as Gracie watched, she thought of herself at their age. She had a crush on a red headed boy name Sonny. He was tall, strong and good looking but by high school was involve in sports trying to show off to us girls and another girl won his heart.

Taking her eyes off the children she examines Joey's face, now a little sweaty and that bowtie gave his clean shaving face a handsome look with his hair cut such he looked like a college kid with his well-built body and those hazel eyes were bluer then normal and when he glanced at her, she could see there was an image of admiration for her and as he turned back to watching the children, his eyes also brought a feeling of trust she has never felt before as he held her hand. Like it belongs there.

The thought cause her to pull his hand loose saying "Restroom" and left Joey not looking back trying hard to control this emotional feeling that was trying to overpowered her at the moment.

"Get control of yourself, girl" is all she was thinking as she entered the restroom.

Now Joey was thinking watching her nicely shape body back walk away, "What a woman? What a great dancer? I think I'm in love. In fact, I know I'm in love."

Then he thought, "I'm going blow this like I've done all the others girls I've known and like Charlie said, "After one date they were never seen to want to go out again."

He was about to laugh as a nice two step began when one of the girls broke his concentration as the girl asked saying, "Mr. Joey, will you please dance with us? There are not enough boys for us to dance with."

Turning to face the girl, he saw it was Betty, the girl that lived down the street who his sister would baby sit now and then when she was younger and done grown up and in his 4th period English class.

Joey gave her a big smile as he said, "Sure" and as he looked past her he could see ten or more girls watching for his answer and looking over at the boys there only four that either could not dance or chicken.

It was a waltz and thanking Mrs. Shoemaker under his breath, he settled into her arms and quickly found out she did not how to slow dance well but was trying. But he thought, "I bet she can fast dance."

As he slowly brought Betty into the rhythm motion and beat of the music, letting her learn the waltz from him and got her dancing to the music, he glanced over at the girls thinking, "I wonder, do I have to dance with all them."

As they waltz into the boy's area Joey stopped asking, "Who would like to take Betty from me?"

"I will," Andy said coming forward and gently took Betty's hand from Joey bringing her to him saying, "You sure are better dancer than me," just before they calmly dance away and Joey wanted to laugh for Andy spoke the truth, "He was a worst dancer then Betty."

But as he turned to leave them, he heard Betty say, "It's easy. Just follow my footsteps like Mr. Joey showed me. It's easy. Here let me show you."

He stopped and watch them a second seeing that Andy was a quick learner caught on quickly what Betty showed him and both were waltzing somewhat when the music stopped. But they remain together on the dance floor discussing his and her dancing abilities.

Joey wanted to laugh watching them remembering somewhat his first dance here at school. He was just like Andy.

Seeing Gracie come out of the restroom he wonder over toward her when Mrs. Shoemaker started an old 50's song he gotten from Grandma who got it couple weeks ago at a last yard sale she went to over in Leslie called, "The Twist."

The beat and words of the song cause the children to go crazy trying to dance the way the song asked them too. So as Gracie join him he called out saying, "Watch me and Gracie it easy."

Joey looked at Gracie saying, "Let's do the Twist for them. You do know how?"

"I sure do," she answered as she gave him a smile and began to twist to the music.

Joey watched her dance a second admiring her beauty and the way she moved to the music before joining her in the twist but his eyes were upon Gracie and in the dimmed lighting, her movements to the music gave her a happy look as if she was really enjoying it and could she ever twist. Quickly the children began to copy her with most either laughing or fussing. Then as the music stopped Mrs. Shoemaker immediately started it again. Which brought on a cheer as the children went back to twisting away.

But Joey reached and caught Gracie's hand and while motioning with his head toward the teacher's setting area, said, "Let's rest and let the Boys and Girl have the dance floor."

Gracie let him hold her hand as they wondered through the dancers toward an empty table and as they neared it, Mr. Treat called out, "Great dancing."

"Thanks," Joey returned as he pulled out a seat for her to sit asking, "Something to drink," before doing a dance move as he held out his right hand toward like saying, "Well."

Gracie could only laugh at his action saying, "If they don't have a Gin and tonic, I'll take any soda they got."

Joey glance at her giving her this "what" look before saying, "I'll be sure to check." He was laughing as he left thinking, "Gin and Tonic, I got to remember that one."

As the music stopped with a loud "Twist away" Maryann interrupted her thoughts on Joey as he walked away when she said, "Isn't he the most marvelous creature you ever seen."

Gracie looked at Maryann and laughed while answering with, "Do I show I'm festinating with him that bad."

Sandra joined Maryann and both were laughing as they said, "Yes."

"Well, you two run along now he is mine," Gracie said with a fake serious sound in her voice.

Maryann placing her arms around Sandra asked almost laughing, "Can't we watch how you win him over?"

"No, now get," Gracie commanded with an added hand motion with it as she turned eyes on Joey as he was returning to bring her a cup of coffee. He was so handsome and Gracie wondered why some girl hadn't already grabbed him. He had a way about him that was charming and he treats me as if I've always been his friend and his long word contest sure has the children talking and he is the best dancer I've ever dance with and his touch as we dance has my body desiring more.

"Dam it what I am to do with Milton?" she suddenly thought as Joey sat her coffee before her added a sugar and a cream package beside it saying, "I thought you would like something hot for I found it cools me down faster and it seems to relax me better after dancing."

After her first drink of the hot coffee she did feel more relax more in control of her emotions over Joey but careful not to show it as she smiled over the cup asking, "It does relax you, thanks but where you learned to dance. You are the best dancer I've ever dance with."

Almost laughing, Joey pointed toward Mrs. Shoemaker as he took a seat saying, "It is all Mrs. Shoemakers fault. I grew up in this school and she made sure we all learn to dance and it seems dancing just came naturally to me. But of all the girls I've danced with since the 6th grade you are by far the best."

"Dance school," is all Gracie answered before lifting her cup up to take a sip, waiting to see his reactions to her words.

Joey gave her a smile as he asked, "Dance school, I guess you were in Baler Let school."

"I did not call it that," Gracie said wanting to laugh as she said, "I called it just The Dance Hall or Nancy's and it was not a Baler Let School or whatever you said."

"Well, tell me all about it," Joey asked as he moved closer to the table then one motion he placed his elbows on the table with face resting in his folded hands looking at her which cause her to smile into those eyes that were almost blue.

Then a "I waiting" broke her thoughts upon his handsome face causing her to say, "Now this girl does not want to give all her secrets away but I will tell you it made me learn how to dance."

Her words cause Joey to sit up straighter with a happy face saying, "Whatever school it was it sure made you a great dancer."

Charlie just catching Joey's last words as he took a seat beside Gracie and as Bill grabbed the other chair, he said, "Gracie went to Dance School alright......."

That is all he got out when Gracie suddenly grabbed him saying, "Now Charlie leave your two cents out of our conversation."

But as she let him said, "Go ahead and tell him for I'm not."

Suddenly, a hopping good Jitterbug song fills the air with Mr. Jinn calling out "Breaks over."

Charlie and Bill quickly left the table with Charlie tapping Gracie on the shoulder saying "Alright, I'll be quiet" and was laughing by the time he caught up with Bill.

Joey watched them leave and as he turned back to Gracie to find her getting out her seat saying, "Come on Joey, let's dance" and that is what they did, liking the feel of each other as they dance. Admiring the way each would twist and turn as they dance the fast dances and all the time the children watched and copied.

As the lights came on and Mrs. Shoemaker played the song she always played as the last song with Elvis singing, "Love me tender Love me blue for I'm in love with you."

The song lit up Gracie's enter feelings for Joey so she smiles at him saying, "Thanks for a great time" and left him before he could respond calling out, "Come on Charlie lets go home."

"Bill's coming," Charlie responded as he caught up with Gracie with Bill right behind him.

Gracie did not answer him as she walked toward the exit she thought, "If I've stayed I know I would have gone home with him. It has been six months since Milton left me for another girl because she had money. He was just a bum looking for a jerk off and I was the sucker."

At the exit, she glances back upon Joey feeling horny and could see him watching her and out of the blue and really could not help herself, blew him a kiss.

Joey reached and acted like he caught the kiss and place it into his heart saying, "Oh no, I forgot to get her phone number" but as he started to run and catch her, Mrs. Shoemaker stopped him saying, "Joey, I have her phone number and I'll give it to you after we clean up. Now grab those two chairs beside you."

As Joey helped Mrs. Shoemaker, Gracie was backing the car out. Her mind was on Joey when Charlie beside gave her a slight push saying, "Bill, Gracie just likes Mr. Joey and she not in love with him yet" then pushing her again asked, "Aren't you Gracie?"

"You two leave me alone," she countered adding, "Quick pushing me." "Bill, your right she is in love," Charlie spoke before busting out in laughter quickly join by Bill from the back seat singing, "Gracie's in love."

By the time Gracie drove into the driveway, she was about ready to kill both boys with their laughter but as she parked, Bill and Charlie became quiet in anticipation of getting out when Gracie asked, "Does it show that bad."

"Yes," both boys said as they left Gracie in the car reaching to get her cell phone from her purse all the while fighting the urge to call him as she dials Joan's number while under her breath said, "Darn their hides."

When Joan answered, Gracie immediate said, "Joan, you never guess what happen at the dance tonight."

"Gracie, you know what time it is," Joan returned.

But Gracie answered with, "I'm sorry if I woke the Baby, I forgot about her. But Joan, I just had to tell you who I met today."

Joan was laughing as she said, "Another boyfriend."

"I'm telling you this is the one I've been seeking for my whole life," she answered.

"What his name," Joan asked and was quickly answered with Gracie saying, "Joey Williams."

There was silence on the other end and as Joan returned laughing, "I know him. In fact, I grew with him and he was the best dancer in school."

"Joan, I've never dance with a man that could dance like him," she serious said. "I mean really I've never met one. What can you tell me about him?"

"I can tell you Joey Williams never dated in school," Joan answered. "He is always saying, "If I date it will be with the one I will marry,"

"Well he asked me out on a date," Gracie answered.

"He did," Joan replied before saying, "Wow, you are the first I know of." Suddenly in the background came the cry of a baby and as it did Joan said, "Got to go its feeding time and Gracie I want to know everything you hear me."

Chapter 5

THE PARKING LOCK WAS FULL OF CARS BY THE TIME JOEY ARRIVED at the Baseball game forgetting they were also having the teams annual Fish Fry whenever they played North Side High and the both communities does show up for Charlie Gram was cooking and can he cook fish.

As he exited his Chevy Sprint, he could see the stands were full and off to his right were those preparing the fish around several tables. He remembers when he was playing third base he had asked Mr. Klenz, who has always been West University's Baseball coach, "Why they had these fish fries" and he answered, "To pay for everything they need to play baseball." He also remembered Mr. Klenz had a way about him that made the team give him their best and as he stopped at the edge of the stands trying to see where Gracie was sitting, he glances across the field and could see Charlie was playing second and the score board showed North Side already had a run and wanted to laugh for the bases were also loaded.

When he started to glance back to the stands, the batter hit the pitched ball into Charlie's glove and all he did was step on second ending the inning with stands giving the kids applause for getting out of the inning alive.

He thought, "Been there, done that more than once" but glancing across the stands he could see Gracie was sitting with some young girls being harassed by the twines Frank and Milton Thomas. Maryann and Sandra were sitting behind her with several other girls who suddenly gave a good yell for the player to run.

His attention turned to the playing field just able to catch the hitter being put out at first. So as he started to head for Gracie thought, "Time sure has change things, Girls never went to any game he played. But maybe it is the Fish Fry is why they are here for."

But he only taken a few steps when Gracie noticed him and left her seat and slowly came out of the stands saying "Excuse me, sorry" as she did.

Joey watched her admiring how she had dress with her long brown hair tied in the back of her head exposing a beautiful face which wore no makeup. She had on a light brown pants and a brown shirt that gave him a very all girl image and once upon the ground run to him and almost threw her arms around him saying, "About time you showed up. I thought I was stuck with Milton and Frank all game."

"Well this was unsuspecting, I do say," Joey answered as he wrapped his arms around her feeling her nicely shaped body against his.

"I told them I had someone coming to sit with me, but them two, would not leave me alone," she whispered in his ear before she exited his arms adding, "and I'm hoping jumping in your arms would give them a message to leave me alone."

Glance back toward the stands he could the twins were following her and as they arrive near them several on those sitting at the stands cry out "Get of our line of sight" or "Hay, your blocking our view" and of course Mr. Snow, who's lawn he mowed a thousand times said, "If you going to fight, do it behind the bleachers" which only brought laughter around them.

Both ignored them as Frank said, "Sorry Gracie. We did know Mr. Joey was your boyfriend."

Both seem to humble themselves as they left them with Gracie calling out, "By boys" wondering why Milton called back saying, "See you around Joey."

Joey did not return an answer and both seem to almost run as they left which cause Gracie to ask, "Joey, why did they seem to be in a rush to leave. Aren't they your friends?"

"Not really," he all he answered as he held out his hand toward her.

Gracie reached and for his hand thinking, "There must be more to this Joey Williams then she thought" and as she took his hand began leaving him back to where she was sitting and even before they took their seat the girls started asking him questions about the Long Word Contest, his life and did he like Gracie and was he going to marry her and many other questions but became quiet when Gracie told them to stop as Bill hit a base hit past second base causing them to join the other mothers and dad's to cheer them on for it seem the West University Wild Cats were getting beat by the score of 1 to 0.

More cheers went up for Charlie to hit a home run as he came to bat and gave a smile back to the stands as swung his bat several times preparing himself for the first pitch which he let pass and of course it was a strike. Took a big swing at the second and missed.

Joey was sure he was going strike out on the third but Charlie hit it foul back into the netting behind him. The Raff threw another ball to the pitcher and after catching the ball, the pitcher seemed to really concentrate on his next pitch which Charlie took a big swing at giving it all his worth and missed.

"Strike three," the Raff called out ending the inning.

As the teams change places, Joey asked Gracie, "Do you like catfish?" "Sure do," Gracie answered looking upon Joey's good looking face and noticed a slight scar on the edge of left eye she had not noticed before.

Joey gave her a smile and just as he started to say more when the stands busted out with yells as the West University's batter hit a base hit into right field so he had to ask over the yelling, "I know a place they'll be serving it right after the game. Would you like to go?"

Then from behind came, "Can Sandra and me I come also?"

"Of course you are coming sillies," Gracie answered before with a smile asked, "I hope you have the money to play for your fish."

"We do," Sandra answered with Maryann saying, "Why don't we leave now. It is the last inning and looks like West University lost 0 to 1 and they have two outs."

"Good idea Sandra," Joey answered and as he stood holding his hand out to Gracie saying, "If we wait for Charlie and Bill, our fish will be cold and I like mine nice and hot."

Gracie took his hand as she stood saying, "Let's go get some fish and the boys fend for themselves."

It seems everyone had the same idea for there was already a long line and there seem to more yelling here than in the stands so the small group join the food line with the four girls leading the way with Maryann joking what kind of fish she wanted saying, "I hope it's hot. I hate cold fish myself."

Suddenly Sandra said, "Save our place Mr. Joey. I see Mother and Dad."

Then turning to the others said, "Come on and let us leave Mr. Joey and Gracie alone."

"Come on Carla an Betty let's leave also," Maryann suggest as she followed Sandra and quickly Joey and Gracie was alone in the food line with Joey calling out saying, "I'd save your place in line and Maryann, you know you can find us easily, we will be at the very end of the line."

Then turning to Gracie, Joey asked, "You been going to all of Charlie's games?"

"Not really," she answered. "Dad and Mom is usually his ride and I go if they can talk me into it. But a fish fry is another story and not only that, I'm to meet a very charming and handsome guy who was supposed to be here, so I caught a ride with them and even put up with that brother of mine who pester me all the way here about you. While Daddy seemed to enjoy Charlie's ribbing and keep getting him to say more."

Then she laughed before saying, "Mostly, Charlie's ribbing was funny and all I could do was laugh with Mom and Dad."

"I can see they love you dearly," Joey said with a smile before thinking, "There is something about her that has gotten my notice and it is reaching into my heart and I know I'm falling in love with her." Then looking up he whispered, "Lord help me."

But Gracie's words brought him back to reality as she said, "What you going to do later on today and tonight?"

Joey thought a second before catching onto her meaning answered with, "I could be sleeping with a real pretty girl is what I'm been thinking about." "Mmmm," Gracie thought before saying, "I'm not that easy my friend to get in bed with I assure you? But, you see I would have to sneak out of the house and I can't do that so let us see what the future holds before we end up in bed together."

Joey was a little humble as he said, "I'm sorry I was so bold but we both know we are going to end up in bed together. Don't we?"

"You'll still bold," Gracie answered and with a smug face said, "But the answer is still "No.""

"Then why did you asked me what I'm going to be doing tonight," Joey asked with a little wondering and wishing.

"I have Choir practice at seven and was wondering would you like to come and watch is all," she answered and then with her best smile said, "Would you?"

Joey looking disappointed asked, "What's the Choir's name?" "We go by the name "Singles Gospel Choir," Gracie answered.

"And all Singles Choir," Joey question before saying, "You mean every singer is single."

"I sure do," she answered before walking around in circles before him half singing "And it made up of male and female singers and we sing those gospel songs. There are singers that you would not believe and little me, stuck in the middle singing tenor with four other single girls that have come and gone with a gold ring on their finger."

Joey laughed at her dancing and her words before saying, "Strange way to say I'm single and looking for a mate?"

"Oh no, you have it all wrong," she answered with a slight whisper to it before boldly saying, "We are singers, Joey. We sing for the joy of hearing our voices coming together singing out praise to our Lord and Savior and in middle of the singing the Spirit of God flows. Come and hear us sing and rejoice with us. I promise we want hurt you?"

By now Joey was getting this I got to see thinking said, "I'll be there but where you be singing at?"

"Church at 1st and 2nd street, the big white church," she answered.

"That's the Church of God," Joey asked thinking what he heard about the church and not that he didn't believe but that Church was too close to God from what he remembered so before saying, "All I can promise you is I'll try to be there."

Suddenly Charlie showed up breaking their togetherness saying, "Got to go, Gracie. Mom and Dad or leaving" then turning to leave said, "Come on Gracie you can see him at choir practice tonight. So come on."

Gracie struggle a second before saying, "Got to go and you promise to be there."

Then as Charlie grabbed her arm pulling her away saying, "Come on," she points at him with the other hand saying, "You better come."

As he watched her being pulled away by Charlie with her fussing, she was coming and him saying, "Come on."

Joey thought, "I can't lose this one as I've done so many others who was like me really looking only for little sex and companionship for a while before we became history. But this girl is different, exciting and beautiful all at the same time. It's like I'm in a trance and my eyes can only stare at her beauty and wondering, "What have I got myself into?"

Then he whispered lightly saying, "So is this what love feels like."

Chapter 6

JOEY ARRIVED EARLY THIRTY MINUTES BEFORE SEVEN TO MAKE SURE she did not worry if he was coming or not and was surprise to find the parking lot was full of cars from old to new with a truck or Van thrown in for measure.

He easily found a good parking spot thinking, "I thought this was going to be small group of singles and it looks like to be hundreds and now I can see why this is a big parking lot."

There were few vocals singing as he followed several other young girls and Guys into the church and seem to be preparing to sing when he saw Gracie with several girls' dress in jeans and blue top as if was a uniform as well as Gracie and all the girls wore their hair in a ponytail.

As the singles began to find a seat at the choir bleachers with seats of old four by eights of raw oak by fours when from a side door came a well dress fairly tall man wearing black pants and colorful shirt and as he walked out before the gathering singers cause a quiet as he called out, "Ok Singers, it is time to practice but as you gain your hard seat remember it is to remind you without a good prayer life in trust that what your ass be doing your whole life."

Then one girl cried out, "Brother William, who you want to start our singing tonight.

There was several "Me's" called out but Brother William went into a unknown language and closing his eyes called out saying, "Not a member of the Choir, a stranger that just walk in to show how this prayer going change people's lives" and as he opened his eyes, he look straight at Joey saying, "You must be the one the Lord wants to start this prayer and song time that has begun tonight and will go not stop for 40 days and nights."

Then he turned to the gathering crying out, "Folks, I want a revival. I want healings, and I want anybody here to know the Baptizing Tanks is always open. This church door's are always open for prayer and tonight we start a forty day none stop prayer and praise for a revival of our community and to start us off a complete stranger to the church will sing us a song.

In the quiet Preacher William asked Joey saying, "I would like you to sing a solo song of praise to God."

Now Joey was in shock to find himself the center of attention and only song he could think of was Amazing Grace so stood before the congregation and began to sing and in him the Holy Ghost bubble up and he could not help it began to cry as he sung which caused Gracie came out of the crowd and began to help him, then another and soon everybody was singing with him and as he finishes many was already Praising God before he had finish singing.

Preacher William gave him a smile saying, "Well done. Now get."

Gracie pulling his arm saying, "You got to get yourself out of the way you are standing in the "Singer's Stop."

Then as another singer began to sing "I was once lost in sin" he realized why Preacher William choose him for he had been standing under a several microphones hanging from the ceiling.

For an hour or two he stood around with Gracie joining into many of the songs and slowly in became nothing but individuals giving praise to God nonstop.

He been going to a Pentecostal Church of God near his house but although the Spirit moved it was nothing compared to this Church Service and he wondered can the church keep going nonstop for forty days. Right now he was sure of it but, "Forty Days was a long time?"

He would just stare at Gracie and watch her as she rejoices in the Holy Ghost when a good rejoicing song would be singing she'll be Jumping around like she was still a young girl. As she sung her long brown hair tied back of her head, bounced with her making her even more radiate to him.

It was either the Holy Ghost or he himself that open his eyes to love and suddenly he was completely in love with her as he watches her sing with a good Christian song being herself. To him she was a very active and fascinated young woman and his friend and he had determined that she made him come here to see who she really was, a child of God and was he willing to date her as such.

"Dam," he thought, "I'm in love and I know I'll never get the image of her dancing so sexy before me showing off."

He could only laugh as she sometimes dances around him running her hand around his body and did the Holy Ghost hit him when she did as if telling him to control himself, "Take her into your arms and kiss her" and as she came around to face him, she looked into his hazel eyes and he could see "yes" as she melted into his arms her eyes which were the sexiest eyes he's ever seen as he calmly kissed her.

It was returned back to him as they kissed until a new song came on that she wanted to dance too and as they parted and still holding her hand, Joey asked, "Do you mind if I enter your life and stay awhile."

She just smiled and it lit her face up as she said, "I wouldn't have it any other way" and with the praises of thanks echoing around them he could see in her eyes she was in love with him or fascinated by him, he wasn't sure.

But to him it looked like love and then a thought hit him, "Here I am preparing to make love with Gracie right here on the floor of the Church."

Then loudly he began to do his Holy Ghost shuffle hollering with the others, "Thank you Jesus" between thinking control yourself idiot, being in real love with a woman for the first time had him shouting "Glory to God" one second and dancing to her in the next.

Somehow he found love for a lovely woman that had become a friend quicker than a snake can hit a rat. He was just plain oh Joey running around and now he a Joey in love and it has thrown him for a loop.

As he calmed down to see Gracie had been watching him shout "Thank you Jesus" she asked, "You seem awful happy right now?"

"Oh, I am, I am," he answered back, wanting, but not wanting to tell her he was in love with her. It was a new feeling in his heart that the Holy Ghost seemed to help amplify into a pure Love for someone. Nothing was faked about this love he felted. It filled him from his groin to this mine and his eyes were filled with the image of her dancing and shouting praises to the Lord until she got harsh and had to have a drink which lead them away from the shouting to the outside for inside was for worship no food are drink.

There Joey found across the back wall was a plywood panels with times and dates across them for people to fill in, when the news people began to show up almost fighting to grab someone and ask about the Great Forty Day nonstop Praise the church is having and that when a Channel 14 Reporter with cameraman following called out to Gracie and Joey as they exited the building with "What a friend we have in Jesus" being sung behind them saying, "Would you please tell Channel 14 viewers about this forty day prayer service Pastor William has started here tonight?"

Joey started to tell him he knew nothing but Gracie spoke up saying, "Sure I'll tell you what he has started. To tell God we love him and thank him for the great salvation he has given us in the name of his only begotten son, Jesus Christ. It is his hope to bring God's eyes upon the city and bring peace upon the broken hearted. He hoping it will bring happiness with love and place in the many hearts that come here to help praise God for forty days."

Then looking straight into the camera said, "This prayer service in not limited to those in the area, if you can know what I mean. Just come and join into the greatest experience you will ever experience. I believe people will be healed before the forty days are up so come choose a time to praise God come in fifteen minutes early before you start if you can and sing and prayer."

The reporter realizing what the Girl had said asked, "Are you saying anyone can come and sing Praise to God these next forty Days?"

"That I am," she answered as the camera man focus on Gracie she continued with, "Just come and write your name on the plywood panels saying when you going be here is all and show up."

As the Reported started to ask another question she stopped him saying, "Before these forty day are up, the church will need your help. So come and joined into Preachers William dream of a forty-day praise to God from our city and be heal at the same time. Already several individuals have been Baptize in the name of Jesus Christ today and if you have not been Baptize come and be bless."

The reporter turns to the camera saying, "You heard it first on Channel 14. So come and join them in Praising God nonstop for forty days and nights."

Catching a chance to leave, they left the reporter who was bragging about the city does need an answer.

Joey was happy and smiling how Gracie handled the saturation they had gotten themselves into and said so saying, "You're going be all over the news. Did you know that?"

"I wasn't thinking when he asked me a question. It just came out is all," she answered picking up couple paper cups and asked, "What your pleasure?"

"Just a coke will do," Joey answered before adding, "The only problem I see is now all the kids at school going to know where I've been tonight."

His words were funny causing her to laugh almost spilling the soda she was pouring from the soda bottle. But as she handing Joey his soda said still laughing, "But I do not think it is going to change your contest one little bit."

"I guess not," Joey said before laughing. "Did you know my Dad was the one who suggested I do this contest with the children? He had all the writing pads run into and old computer system and even had his helpers Mutt and Jeff bring it to the classroom and set it up for me."

"That is not their real name's is it, Mutt and Jeff," Gracie laughed.

Joey joined her laughter before saying, "Yes that is their name believe it or not."

Charlie interrupted their conversation as he came running up saying, "Mom and Dad want to know you riding home with Joey, if not then come on their leaving."

Gracie thought a second before looking at Joey who had a sad face already knowing her answer as she said, "Run along Charlie and don't forget about Bill. I'll be along in a minute."

But Charlie had to say as he left, "Mr. Joey, see you Monday and Maryann said, "The sixed period class is going to win and we also going to win the grand prize" and was just a laughing as he ran back inside dodging the reporter and his admirers answering questions.

Joey turned his attention to Gracie and could see she was thinking. So he remained quiet looking at her, the girl of his dreams he thought. So beautiful, witty and her smile just lights up her face and those glorious eyes of hers always looking at him and he could see Love in them for him. She must feel as I do from all her actions and caring. But it almost tore his heart out when she said, "Remember be here fifteen minutes early before you sing a song. You can even sing one you written, English Professor. But I got to go and I do not go home with a boy I just met."

But Charlie appeared again from around the corner saying, "Come on sis, we got to go, their leaving."

Without another word but "Love you," Gracie quickly followed at a slow run having to dodge several singers seemly getting ready to go on stage.

He follows her around the corner and saying to himself, "I'll be seeing you for you got my heart and are not getting away from me girl."

Watched his love run away, it almost broke his heart as she did. The night air filled with car lights and very little outside lighting made her looked very defensiveness and sign with relief as she entered her Mom's and Dad's Dodge Van and as she did she waved at him and threw him a kiss which he instantly threw back as she disappeared and they drove off.

Walking toward his car he felt alone. Her attitude on life was puzzling to him. She had his heart and it was fighting to stay or run like he did all the others girls he known. But he never felt this way about a girl and as he sat down at the driver's seat said, "It must be love for I can't get her out of my head.

It was close to midnight when Joey entered his fully furnished apartment. This was the second day of spending the night there still having a room at home and he was tired and excited at the same time over Gracie.

"Unlike any Pentecostal girl I've met," Joey thought as he open the fridge reaching for the already made ice cream cones, he said, "Just what I need to relax my mind over Gracie. She got me all screw up in my love thinking."

As he opens the Nutty Buddy, Joey saw his guitar leaning against the small lounge chair and thought, "Good idea William let's play."

Throwing the wrapper away, washed his hands and all the while thinking of a song he could play that just maybe reflex his feelings for Gracie. He kept thinking, "I've never felt this way toward a Girl before. I mean the getting married having children and living everyday with women in my bed? It has crossed my mind a lot lately and I know I must be in love. What else could it be the way I feel inside right now, all crazy inside, thinking one way going the other?"

As he grabbed his guitar, Joey sat down saying, "Lord Help me I need your strength to live through this with Gracie who I'm seeing her as my love and I feel will be my wife. I just met her and I'm confused at my feelings for her but in my heart I know she has feelings for me and I wonder if their just as bad."

Picking a couple strings, he said, "This is you Gracie" and began to play Wildwood Flower.

Chapter 7

AROUND EIGHT THAT MORNING JOEY'S MOM CALLED SAYING, "I hope you awake by now. I like her and if you don't marry her I will. Did you know you and her are all over the news?"

"Mom I just woke up," he answered as he stood heading for the bathroom. "Go to Channel 14 and see," she returned before saying, "Bye, remember church" then he heard silence as she hung up on him and his thinking, "Must be something good and juicy on TV for her not to hound him about something he knows he did not do."

Turning on the TV he caught the image of him and Gracie sneaking off away from the Reporter who was going crazy with the commentator saying, "After giving such wisdom she sneaks off for a soda which I believe is more important than standing before me answering questions."

Joey laughed as he fixed himself something to eat thinking, "I wonder if I could see her today and make it look like that I'm not chasing after her like the dog heat I'm in, but, how can I act like I'm not?"

After a shower and dress in his Sunday best he left the apartment with guitar in hand heading for Church and upon entering there was Gracie talking to Mom in a corner where no one could hear them Mom was moving her hands about in excitement as they talked.

Joey watched a second before thinking, "If she going to get Mom to help her win me over. I guess I better play along and see what happens."

As he set up his guitar placing it on the stand, Gracie walked toward him saying, "Please don't be mad at me. Your singing at my church talked me into returning the favor of visiting my church. I thought I come and see what your Church is like and I like it."

"Am I glad to see you," Joey answered.

Looking at him in her funny face asked, "You're just glad to see me is all." Laughing he answered, "Oh no, I'm way more than just glad but it fits the picture."

Then he gave her a bow saying, "I'm very glad to see you. Is that better?" Then stepping off the stage reached and pulled her to him saying, "Or should I take you in my arms saying, "Hal-a-Lula, Baby. Am I glad to see you?"

Laughter broke out between them and those watching.

As they separated Gracie looked so petite said, "Now how can this girl get a good reputation in this Church when I'm being swung around by a good looking man as you are."

Smiling he answered saying, "Well you asked "If I was just Glad and I answer you the best way I know how," Then with a little bow said, "Would you like to join the small music group we have here and sing a little praise to our Lord and savior?"

"I sure would," she answered but the one became two and by the sixth song she gave crying, "No more songs please from me and I know almost all the songs in this song book. I started singing with Amazing Grace and memorize very song in this book by I was ten. Just pick a song and for God I will sing one more for you."

But she was looking at Joey waiting for his song and looking into those cool dark eyes of hers said, "Just One Rose Will Do."

Tears came into her eyes as she begun to sing and really flowed as she sung out, "Just one rose will do."

As she finished the whole church exploded with applause and tears as the love between the two exploded before them as he finished the song with a few notes and strums on his guitar.

After the service Joey's Mom had a fit over Gracie while his Dad asked, "I've seen you chase girls all your life and this one seen to have captured your heart and hearing her sing I can see why?"

Joey looked at his father who advice he always took asked, "Dad, she got me all strewed up inside and I'm not sure what I should do?"

Joey's Dad shook his head saying, "The only answer I can give, I would marry her in few months or tomorrow if she would let me."

"But Dad," he said as his Father turned and left him saying, "That what I would do and suggest you do the same."

Joey just laughed enjoying his Dad's acceptance of Gracie.

Looking at his Mother and Gracie, he didn't have to worry about Grandpa or Grandma for they are out of the picture and in his thinking thought he should go see them when Gracie said, "I just love your Mother."

Joey wondering where her ride was for a second boldly said, "I guess she told everything she knew about my exploits and failures."

"Oh no," she answered, "I don't think your name come up once in our conversation."

With only Mr. and Mrs. Waid left to leave the parking lot Joey looked at Gracie asking, "Where your ride?"

Giving him her little girl looked answer with a smile saying, "Why, you are." Joey just smile as he answered saying boldly, "I was wondering is all and hoping with the other that you had no ride."

Opening the passenger door, he looked at this remarkable woman asking, "Where do you suggest I take you?"

Taking his hand to help her she slid into the seat saying, "Let's go walking on the beach? You choose which one?"

"Good Idea," Joey answered as he closed the car door and was he excited and laughing as he took a seat to drive.

As he started the car, Joey said, "If we'll going swimming, I better stop and get my swim trunks?"

"That would be a good idea," she answered giving him her best sexy smile. They made small conversation as he drove toward his apartment and she just watched him from the time he backed the car out drove. Admiring his handsome face with his curly hair cut short around the ears and clear shaving gave him the image of greatness in it and his smile was a joy to see with clean white teeth.

All, his Mom would say about him was "He will take care of you and your children" and she never will forget his Mom's smile that she gave when she said it. But somehow he has become her fascinated and his manor was always with honor and suddenly whispered saying, "It just as Mom said to do, "Never ride in a car alone with a guy unless you were going to marry him" and here I am with Joey, alone, so by our Load's Grace I guess I'll marry him."

Joey pulling into the driveway on M-street broke her admiring of him to saying, "I want to change before we go swimming and I can do that in your apartment is that alright with you?"

Before he could answer, she was out the door and half way up the stairs.

He could see she was in a rush to see inside but never thought she'll wanted to see his apartment this bad and as he exited the car from the balcony above Gracie called out saying, "Come on."

"The door is open," he called back thinking, "Dam, I hope all my smoke is put upped."

She entered and headed for the bathroom not sure how to handle the situation she got herself into. But I am going to sleep him of course which only enhance the lustful feeling she was dealing with at the same time. She liked sex and the feeling of a penis in her moving, in and out, back and forth.

"Dam it, stop that thinking girl," she said to herself as she quickly changes into a bathing suit and in her eyes it gave her body a very female appearance then as she places her stuff in her bag said, "In heat I hope."

When she opened the door, she caught Joey getting ready to undo his pants causing him to quickly stopped saying, "Sorry Gracie, thought you would be in there little longer."

Feeling the lust in her she said, "Let me help you. If I'm going to sleep with you I like to see what you got to offer me."

Joey was in shock as she came to him and looking into the eyes began to undo his belt and slowly as she unzipped his pants she felt his hard penis against her hand only increase her lust for him to fuck her and she had learned as a child, "If you want a honey man all she had to do was to become the aggressor."

As she ran her hand across his hard and strong belly feeling the tension he was in over her touch so she said, "Calm down now I'm not going to bite you. You see, for the man I'm going to live with the rest of my life, I would like to first explore a little of him, don't you think?"

"Well I," is all he got out before she pushed him onto the bed saying as she sat down beside him saying, "Before some friends drugged me down to Brother William's Church I was a young beautiful whore who likes to fuck. I still do but have not been with a man ever since the Lord filled me with his Holy Spirit and I want you so bad I can taste it. But to show God I trust him I will not have sex with you until we really get to know one another and I'll be glad to beat you off you want me too."

But his reply caused her to bust in laughter as he said, "Sure, how about in you?"

Suddenly the phone ringing changes their attitude as he quickly grabbed it as his Mother said on the recorder, "Joey you have thirty minutes till your singing take your guitar." But he missed her.

"Darn, where did the time go," he said as he stood pulling his underwear and pant sat back down on the bed frustrated and Horny forgetting he had promise Dad and Mom he would change his time to 3pm instead 7pm as his singing time like other times. He did it just so they could hear him sing before they travel to their church.

Turning to Gracie, Joey very sadly said, "Why don't you spend the night with me latter since I'm going to marry you? You already have my heart and my balls but I must keep my singing time for Brother Williams. So let's get dress, we have plenty of time for sex in the next fifty years of our lives."

As she stripped before him to put on her Sunday going to meeting Pentecostal dress she only wore to Church said, "I do see God's hand in this day for I cannot spend the night with you. Mom and Dad expect me to go home with them tonight."

"Can't you drive," Joey asked as he replaced his nice shirt for one he wore everyday walking out the door and stopped as she answered, "I've never driven a car in my life and never had the need for one."

"You mean you have no driver license," Joey asked a little shocked but understood as she forcefully said, "Sure don't. I have an ID card is all and I'm telling you right now I have no desire to drive a car."

They did not talk as he drove toward Brother William's Church of God but now and then looked at each other and burst into laughter filling the flow of love the Spirit gave.

Joey took a seat under the mikes that was slightly swinging with the air conditions flowing lightly down upon the stage and as soon as the light came on to sing he sung one of his Dad's favorite songs, "What a Stranger."

Chorus:
Yes, God only knows what a stranger has done.
Only God knows who that stranger to be
I was lost and undone until he came along
And the kind words of this stranger set me free

★★

I was so lost in the swamp feeling all bog down
Million of Mosquito's seem to be pushing me around
When this strangers words echoed as I was about to drown
And I'll be bless, if he didn't place me upon solid ground

As I lived and played between the save and the lost
Wondering between my cross and his crown
And no matter how far I wondered when peace I did sought
And I'll be bless, if he didn't place me upon solid ground

Now my feet want to stray with all my wondering ways
Wondering when the trumpet will sound
For I see clearly how much for my soul he had to pay
And I'll be bless, if he didn't place me upon solid ground

Chapter 8

H E CLEARED HIS MIND AS HE WALKED INTO THE CLASS ROOM knowing his thoughts would return to her later but right then he had to get the system up and running before 1st period comes in.

As he checked things out, his mind kept going back to Gracie and her walk in the Spirit of God. He had met Gracie this morning and over a cup of coffee she asked was he ready for his Long Word Contest which he answered said, "I am as soon I get to class and make sure everything was plugged in working."

Watching the screen go through the program runs and soon as screen settled to the game screen. Joey took a seat as the first child came into the room and her manner and glasses made her look like a wise young girl.

Quickly several boys came in disrupting the morning calm as they raced to get a seat in the rear next to each other.

As the other children followed, all their talk was on the game and the length of word and as Joey started to shut the door in walk in the Children's Boss as they called him when he went to school here, Mr. Haydown.

Joey could tell he was getting old and he always knew the name of every kid in school. How was always the question?

But as Mr. Haydown gave Joey a smile as he looked the class over saying, "I'm going be right down the hall and I better be hearing you shouting for that makes you slow and it confuses the guy trying to write a long word down but from the look of you today I bet you can win this game but to win this game your going have do it quietly so the guy writing the long word does not get confuse between wanting to shout Hal-la-lu-la or write the word the down he done forgot."

Turning from the class saying all he was going to say to them but as he walked passed Joey said, "Grown up to be a smart man. Good for you."

But he did not stop to get a response from Joey and Joey did not answer for Mr. Haydown was deaf. He knew one thing Mr. Haydown did enforce the no cussing rule in school and he could read lips from one end of the hallway to the other and you never know when he be watching the sixth grade hallway or any of the others.

Joey looked at the hungry faces ready to start the game saying, "Now that was a great surprise, for as I know, that is the first time that Mr. Haydown ever spook to a class. Like never?"

Walking to the black board he wrote class and under it placed a 1– 6 downward but continued saying, "Shoot you should be honored to be the only class so why don't you gave him an applause and honor him with afoot stomp."

Several girls hollered out, "Foot stomp, what do you mean."

Almost laughing he said, "We had a teacher we all thought was in love with him and to get Mr. Haydown to fetch her something she would have the class stomped the floor for a minute and shortly, Mr. Haydown would appear all smiles."

His words brought laughter but quickly quieted as he wrote Possible Word Length you will be doing the next 10 days. Then over the chatter of the children he wrote, "4, 6, 8, 10, 12, 14, 16, 18, 20, 24" and as he finished, Joey pointed toward the small book shelf saying, "If you will have noticed I have placed a tin can with your class number on it and in your can are the numbers I written on the blackboard."

Then facing the Class saying, "At each class period one of you will draw one number and that will be the words you will write for that class? Now choose?"

In the quiet that followed the wise girl that came in first, said, "I will do it."

The class exploded with many "Yea's."

But the class became quiet as she stood and slowly walk toward that tin can and without looking she picked out a card that had a small red six written with Class 1 written across the top which cause the class to cheer her for her draw many thinking she would draw out the one with read "twenty-four."

As Joey turn to write the number 6 on Class 1 name said, "I need couple volunteers to pass out the dictionaries please and let us get this game a going and who wants to be the handsomest boy in this class room all day?"

The Wise looking girl stood and said, "Bobby you do it."

Bobby was one of the tall skinny kids around and Joey was sure he'll be playing basketball next year in Jr high for he was as tall as he was at six foot two.

Laughter exploded as three boys fought over passing the dictionaries out but Joey did not stop the action as the dictionaries got pass out anyway with much laughter.

"Clear your desks of all pens and writing material, "In four minutes at twenty-five after we will start and you will finish when the class bell rings. You will be able to finish the word you have started but there will be no more and."

Then he pointed to the big TV saying, "And if you fill the whole TV up with words the hold class will get a reward and in each number you will need a hundred words."

Edward took he seat looking the class other and he could see all the kids where ready with a word in mind to write when the Wise Girl stood and said, "We will do this in a orderly way," when the Bell wrong she stopped her yelling and rushed to the key pad to place her word "Driver" on it and answered the question "What did it mean?"

There was some order to their inputs and when the class bell rung stopping the writing. Joey was surprise the kids didn't fill the screen but the repeated words began to kill them, still they came real close to filling the TV screen within thirteen words would have done it.

As the kids grabbed their school books and notes to leave, Joey wrote 87 in the word column and letting their actions be the voice as they left and he could hear the excitement and morning out in the hallway especially about not filling the screen.

Couple guys following couple girls had just left when the next class began to roll in and as they sat began exchanging the class room dictionaries for one they like and the boys in the rear getting stuck with the remains.

But as children sat, he could tell the leader of this group was a guy as he placed his concept of how they were going to win the contest before his class mates he began to repeat "We are the greatest Class #2" and did it with a beat.

But Mary Ann stuck her head crying out, "Class number 6 is the greatest." Joey had to laugh at the explosion of "No ways," rippled across the class." After all the "no way" shouts, the Class settled down as Joey repeated his 1st Period Class statements a smile as the big mouth kid reached into their canned and pulled a 10 out.

There were shouts of joy and sadness at the same time but quickly settle down to quiet as the kids prepared digging into the dictionary to begin and when they left the room Joey was writing by the 10 letter word fifty-four which he was thinking was good when Gracie stuck her head saying, "How it was going?"

"Going great so far," he answered calmly trying not to show he did not want to see for her. He had just got himself calm enough to live with himself and here she is sending his heart into pieces again but he was able to act normal saying, "Figured out a way they could not cheat from one class to the next."

Gracie now real close to him asked, "How did you accomplish that?" Then as she ran her hands across his shoulders feeling him melt under her touched he answered, "Not having two classes do the same word length word is how."

Suddenly the bong for the next class rang out breaking up their time together Joey watched her leave and his heart sank as she walk away giving him a sweet smile and a wave and he was sure she was laughing as she entered the hallway.

He was hoping she'll come back as the first student for 3rd period came into the room from the "potty break" the kids called it sense he started school as it was called. The third period drew 14 and he placed a 48 beside their time slot.

The fourth period class drew 8. Were very fast and more organized and came close to filling the TV Screen with eighty-three words.

At Lunch he set with Gracie where they tried to make small talk about the Contest but it was hopeless for both of them as they hands touch and then she asked Joey, "What you doing after school?"

Joey looked a little sad as he answered saying, "I was thinking of just laying around my apartment and thinking about you is what I think I'll be doing."

Then as she stood for her class, she whispered in his ear saying, "Can I come home with you then we both can think of each other."

As she left the table, the inside of Joey leap with joy understanding her meaning followed her with, "Sure can."

"Good," is all she said as she ran into Charlie standing just outside the door asking, "You going marry him for I never seem you act this way with other guys you dated? I think you are in love with Mr. Joey is what I think."

Looking hard at Charlie she gave her most serious face said, "You better be quiet and do not tell Mom or Dad and that goes double for your buddy Bill."

Chapter 9

GRACIE LEFT CHARLIE THINKING, "DAM AM I RUSHING THINGS just jumping in bed with him?" but Charlie got her thinking as he said, "Gracie, I give him till next Friday to dump you?"

His words cause her to stop and turning back with a little pride to her little brother said, "My love life is nothing you should worry about. You hear me?"

Laughing Charlie found Bill at his locker getting his next period books telling him about Gracie being with Charlie won't last which Bill disagreed saying, "But I think it is love at first sight and I wonder if that will ever happen to me?" then he seems to melt saying, "Love at first sight."

"I wasn't thinking but I can understand what you mean somewhat," Charlie answered as he led the way toward their room and there was Mary Ann telling everyone that entered they could win Mr. Joey's contest.

As they drew close Charlie said, "She will never change. Always be in other people's business, bossy but kind as if she was acting like my Mother always making sure I did not get hurt doing some wild action and I always did and she would come to my aid and help me up and she loved to dance and here she was routing and acting like the Boss" then laugh saying, "But she is the Boss if she can get away with it and this game sure has brought out Mary Ann's best side."

"That it has," Bill answered and were laughing as they came before her, Mary Ann gave them her best smile saying, "Just be calm and cool and we can win Mr. Joey's Long Word Contest."

But Charlie shut her up crying out saying, "I declare you as the one that will draw from the Tin Can for our six period's class."

There was many, "I's" from inside the room inside and continue which made Mary Ann blush as she watched Charlie and Bill move into Mrs. Shoemaker Math Class and her blush became redder as under her breathe said, "Darn his hide."

Charlie left Bill to sit where Mrs. Shoemaker had him seat separating him from Bill. He didn't mine for he got to sit by Mary Ann and as the math teachers always done to him, place a kid strong in a subject to help the one that was weak to understand?

He never minds helping his class mates achieve a good grade. But at times he wasn't sure Mary Ann played dumb in math to get him to be force to sit beside her. She became his friend right off and allowed him and Bill to jump rope with her and Sandra since first grade. Other boys tried but were forced to move on but they let him and Bill jump rope now and then but not when they wanted but when they saw our sad faces did the job to let them jump rope with them and since when Mary Ann and Sandra had learned to swing double ropes, both him and Bill mastered that also when and if they could get them to swing the two ropes. But only Bill could master dodging the two ropes during a hand stand and Charlie had to admire the punishment he endured when they first stated to jump rope in the first grade and started the hand dodging thing and even the two ropes where he really got punish and at times Charlie thought he would scream.

Looking over at where Bill had sat down beside Barbara and Sandra thought a second thinking, "Yep oh Bill going to be a pistol for sure and Mrs. Shoemaker haven't decided who get who or she thinks and figures those three are a lost cause."

He was laughing as Mary Ann took a seat beside him and as Mrs. Shoemaker did her thing she did at the start of every class calling out, "Quiet."

But then she didn't go right into solving some math equation on the Board behind her said, "Every class before you has gone from here into Mr. Joey's Long Word Contest and as I wish the others as I wish you the "Best of Luck."

But Charlie knew what she meant when she continued after a pause saying, "That way I'm the equal between the teams and the one that will be the winner will be the one my Wish was answered?"

Her words only brought laughter among the children understanding her meaning being their math teacher all their school life that she was just wishing everyone "Good Luck" on the start of the contest and it will be her last good luck also for once the game starts what she wishes means nothing in her view. Just like on test days, she always said the same thing to every class, "I wish you the Best of Luck?"

Mary Ann was quiet as she followed the other students into Mr. Joey's class and after she had placed her books away stood by her seat and waited till everybody was took several steps toward Mr. Joey saying, "On behalf of the Six Grade Council which I as the President of want to thank you for giving us something different and has cause us to learn many words we will never use."

Then she bowed and Charlie was shook to hear her thank Mr. Joey for the contest but that all ended as she cried out, "Number six is the best" and as she repeated the phase they began to tapped their feet on the ground and they almost instantly became quiet as Mr. Haydown enter saying, "You called."

But seeing the children laughing at his sudden appearance cause his to give them his evil smile saying, "I can see this class going to be last if they do a lot of banging and screaming but then, the greats can function under such noise."

Turning he walked out the door knowing there was laughter as he left. He like many in this six period class who were always testing his endurance to not put them in the Jailhouse.

After Mr. Joey's speech on what they can and can't do and Mary Ann became the prettiest girl in the class room walked to the can and reaching in, pulled the 20 letter word card.

Instantly Joey heard them begin to open their dictionaries as the Class instantly began looking for a twenty letter word in them and at the clock struck twenty-five and five minutes later Charlie found and his first 20 letter word and when attempted to write it misspell it and had to go back and make sure he spell it right and next time he was able to write Counterdemonstration correctly and his third word of Radiopharmacertarians as The class bell rung out ending the game without Charlie finding another word and as he and Bill left the room Charlie asked, "I wonder what a 24 letter words looks like" but stopped long enough to watched Mr. Joey write Twenty Eight on their Six Period record for twenty letter word which he said was outstanding as class ended.

As Charlie and Bill walked their bikes across the school yard, they were quiet until about halfway to the exit, Bill said, "I only found one word and the words I did find were already used and I did find a lot of sixteen and eighteen letter words."

Charlie understanding what Bill meant busted out in laughter quickly joined by Bill.

Meanwhile back at the classroom, Joey was shutting the word pads computer down when Gracie walked in carrying her purse and a big smile saying, "It looks like you've gotten your second day of contesting over and is still alive."

"That I have," he answered lifted himself up off the floor and as he looked upon Gracie his heart expresses its self in the smile he gave, asking, "If you are ready to leave let's go?"

"We must go by the house first and let me pick up a few things," she answered as she began to turn around and around in front of him displaying her beautiful dress she continued with, "And you don't expect me to wear this dress everyday now do you and I have none at your place."

Joey just smiled thinking, "Dam, give her an inch she takes a mile for in her thinking she has done move in when I said, "Sure?"

Then walking around the table, Joey took her hand saying, "If I'm going to be the love of your life shouldn't you know something about me?"

She pulled her hand back saying, "What I know about you could write a book and I do not need to tell me about yourself. I'm the take it as it is kind of women and I like what I see so I take you as you are with no addends or labels. But then you can call me spoil, rotten and a bad inference on others if you like and will for that is what Daddy tell others about me."

Joey could not help it and busted out in laughter as she began to do a sexy hip movement as she walked toward the door saying, "Let's get on road. I don't want Daddy to know I've moving out."

Chapter 10

As Joey drove up to Gracie's Dad's house, there stacked beside the driveway were all her clothes on top of several boxes and upon seeing it, Joey said, "I guess Mom and Dad already knew?"

"Well I didn't tell them if that what you're thinking," Gracie answered as she left the car stopped and looking over the hood said, "I guess I did tell them when I ask them "Do not enter my room or else.""

After they loaded her clothes Gracie sat in the car and cried, "Just because I had already pack my stuff and my dresses were laying across the boxes, they decided to help us by bringing my stuff down to the street saying, "Bye don't come back?""

"Oh do I love you Joey," is all Gracie said as she began to cry again.

Joey stood outside looking upon Gracie not sure how to handle her crying.

Then he thought, "Holding her want work but if want hurt either" but as he started to walk around the car Gracie said, "Just get in and drive me home and take a long way to get there and let the drive calmed me down."

After backing out and driving down the road, Joey tried to touch her and she quickly took his hand, which seemed to instantly calm her as she said, "Joey you are the third man I've left home with and the other two took me back home the next day because it just didn't feel right. But never was my clothes placed out on the sidewalk before either."

Joey laughed before saying, "I guess your parents are thinking, "Third time is a charm" or something like that?"

His words broke her crying spell and suddenly Gracie began to rejoice crying out the window, "I'm free, I'm free."

Then she turned to Joey saying, "I'm free to love who I want and I want you Joey."

Her words broke his heart and his love for her exploded into crying as he said, "Be quiet darn you?"

His tears soon turned to laughter as his joy and her joy of being together over wham them and began to exciting talked about buying a house, and eventual it got down to kids which stopped for as he parked the car they could see Bill and Charlie peddling their bikes toward them. Acting not sure they should be here.

But Joey calmed their nerves as he exited saying, "I just knew you two would be here to help your sister move into her new home."

Charlie answered him saying, "When I got home and saw where Mom and Dad had moved you out of the house. I went and got Bill to help you move her in?"

His words cause everybody to burst into laughter with Gracie saying, "You'll miss me I just know you will?"

She took the jokes Charlie and Bill made about her moving out of Mom's and Dad's house and moving in with Joey was some good ones and it only made her laugh the more for they could not destroy the Love she felt for Joey right then as he helped her carry her dresses inside. Charlie and Bill took the boxes following.

And Charlie as he followed said, "You know Bill I am sure Gracie is in love or wants to get away from me and made ideas on how she could win a man." Bill laughed before saying, "You offered her advice. Now Charlie, are you telling me you're some kind of expert on the subject of dating?"

"Oh no," Charlie answered before saying, "Now I wouldn't call me and expert but I do know a thing or two about being a guy. You know what I mean?" "Did you know what I told her," Charlie asked taken a better hold of the boxes he was carrying.

Bill following did the same as he asked, "No what?"

Charlie clear his throat before saying, "I told her the next guy she meets, take all your clothes and set them beside the driveway and when you come a get a few things, her clothes be waiting to load."

Bill just laughed saying, "You didn't tell her that, it was your Dad's words for I heard him say that hundred times to her I bet."

But Gracie called back saying, "Quick telling garbage both of you, for I want you to know it was Mother's idea."

Laughter exploding in the car and as it settles Gracie said, "Mom said that how she caught Dad."

Again laughter filled the hallway and continued as they enter Joey's apartment and with Joey's help Gracie was move in with the boxes place where she needed after looking inside. Bill and Charlie just sat on the bed before laying on it watching Gracie put her stuff ready and when she kicked Joey out of the Bathroom saying, "Food?"

Her words cause Charlie and Bill to jump out of bed saying, "We got to go."

Joey watched them leave but food was on his mind when out of the Bathroom came Gracie saying, "All I had to do is mention Food and it reminded them to better get home if they wanted to eat supper."

"Do you want to go out and eat," Joey asked as she stopped and gave him a kiss saying, "Oh no we are not going out to eat, I'm going fix my famous meal known throughout four counties as the best frozen dinner ever made."

"What," he asked.

Then reaching end the bottom of the box brought out a large frozen self-rising pizza from Happy Pappies Pisa over on Tenth Street.

Joey just smiled asking, "I see you got their super special pizza with extra cheese?"

"I sure did," she answered leaving him to turn on the oven.

Charlie watched her move and work, looking in drawers and cabinets and saw she smile at him seeing piles of mismatched dishes with several everyday dishes set on the left side with paper plates.

He could see she was going to make it her kitchen growled out, "stay out." But came back out, saying, "It is too close to the time for you to sing we got to go."

Joey was able to park the car and enter the building just several minutes before his time at seven and a cheer went up at his and Gracie's appearance.

Walking toward the microphones Joey could hear many individuals constantly giving glory and praise to God and as Gracie took a seat beside him, he opened his guitar cast and with a quick tone waited giving Gracie a smile saying, "Thanks for staying with me."

But she answered with, "But where else can I go if not with you."

Joey just gave her a smile as the one in charge pointed raising one finger, then two then on the third finger Joey began to play "I once was lost but Jesus took me in" with Gracie and several others joining in and as the song finish Joey began another of his Dad's songs,

Pharaoh cried, "Hotter, Hotter"
The fire was hot the coals were burning
Red Flames were shooting to the sky
Then as they cast me into the Fire,
I heard the Pharaoh cry

Chorus
Hotter, Hotter, Hotter
Did I not cast in three?
Hotter, Hotter, Hotter
For I see four

They took my hands and they took my feet
And into the Red flames I flew
I flipped and flopped toward the coals
Still hearing the words the Pharaoh cried

I landed unhurt upon the coals
Thinking this could not be
Then I heard the words "Come walk with me"

And I took the hand of the one who set me free

After staying and joining in the singing a couple more hours, Joey took a seat in the small living room and turn the TV on, which it to Roku and hit Pandora bringing forth love songs from Bing Crosby's and other singers and leaning back in the chair all comfortable he watches Gracie prepare their Pisa Meal at times she would dance to the music. Her body she exposes to him as she danced always giving him a smile as after setting the timer she walked out into the middle of the room and holding out her hand said, "Let's dance to this lovely music you have on."

He instantly left the chair and moving it the chair out of the way took Gracie's hands and adjusted his body to hers began to lead her into a slow waltz following the rhythm of the music.

They dance till the pizza bell rung and after eating with small talk they washed their hands, Joey turned off the rooms lights and turning back together continued to dance in the dark.

As they danced, Gracie release her hands letting him hold her and she began to unbutton his shirt, which he did even not try to stop and as she finished, he stopped dancing reaching and did the same to her blouse exposing her bare firm breasts which he felt for a second and as he toss her blouse aside she came real close to him letting her tits do the talking for her as she rub them against his bare chest as they began to dance, she feel his hard on in his pants with its firmed shape against her hip giving her desire for it to be in her.

Sharply she stopped dancing and began removing her skirt saying, "I never could dance with a dress on."

Gracie kickoff her shoes and shortly was standing before Joey only in her underwear and after a couple moves said, "I feel free now like I could dance for at least thirty more minutes before I have to jump in bed to get warm back up."

Joey kicked his shoes off and as he was about to undo his belt Gracie stopped him saying, "Let me take your pants off."

Not moving Joey stood still as she slowly undid his belt then his pants button and as she unzipped his pants she let his hard penis stand out in his underwear and after Gracie pulled his pants off when a real slow Big Band waltz began to play and as she stood tossing the pants into a corner they touch hands and began to dance feeling each other's naked bodies and slowly and loving the feel Joey danced them into and then held her as they collapse onto the bed moving into a good hard sexual tongue fighting kiss.

They did not move each afraid the separation would destroy their inner feeling of love and lust all mixed together into a feeling so strong it seem to drive them together as they felt of each other's body moving from the legs to the face where a kiss had to be performed before they could explode the more. Each taking their time letting the other's body grow in their mind's, the feel of it, the smell, the kissing and the touching as they wondered liking the feel and the shape of each and often enter the panties to touch and feel the her groin and eventually the underwear was removed and into sex they went with pushing and shoving as they tried to obtain as much pleasure out of each stroke as they could and as Gracie was having her third organism Joey exploded in his and morn the sensation was almost too much for him to handle.

As they settled on the bed allowing the sexual lust to calm down, Gracie finally spoke saying, "I diffidently enjoyed that."

"I sure did," he answered as she felt her move to lay her head on his chess.

Then as he placed his hand on her back, pulling her closer she said, "You are not the first guy I've had sex with but this time there was love in it and not just lust alone. I always wanted to have sex and I had a boyfriend in high school and we had sex and instantly I became a whore to him as if my goal was to fuck every guy in school which I assure you I didn't. In fact, you're the first guy since for I made a decision after him to only have sex with the one I love and I do love you"

She cried which brought tears into Joey's eyes as he held her for his love for her was being fed with her feelings.

In the quiet that followed their loving for each other seem to that a rest and they discuss their future and in their conversation, marriage came up and Joey said, "Why don't we do it in front of the sixth grade class at school have a barbeque. Invite our parents of course just to see them fight over us. I know a preacher that would love to do it and he is not affiliated with either of our churches. Not their might be hundreds there to cheer us on into a life, of kids, diapers, and fun."

His words brought laughter among them at the joy of being together over wham them.

Chapter 11

A S JOEY ENTERED THE NEXT DAY'S CLASS, HE WAS QUITE HAPPY and was singing, "Oh happy days" as he prepared the word pad system for class. To him, last night sleeping with Gracie was a dream come true.

"She so beautiful," he said as the first kid entered the class room who brought him back to reality when she asked, "Who's beautiful?"

"My love and my sweetheart," he answered as he looked upon the Wise Girl who came in first yesterday.

"Oh," the girl said and was laughing as she placed her books in her seat. Soon the room was full and the prettiness girl chosen for roll count the Wise Girl without asking pulled a 10 and as the children settle to looking in the dictionaries Joey said, "We will start at 15 instead of 25 from now on. I can see you will need more time to fill the screen up and when it is done you can stop looking and you will win a surprise which will be given at the end of the contest."

He wrote a 83 on their record for their 10 letter word and was late for lunch answering a few question for the Fourth Period class had drew a 6 and had filled the TV screen with still ten minutes left on their time and they wanted to know what they won and all he could say was at the end of the contest they will know.

When he entered the lunchroom, Gracie was waiting, drinking a soda and seeing her beauty, it melted his heart as he grabbed a quick bite and as he sat down beside her said, "Fourth Period class drew a 6 and filled the TV and I forgot the time answering their questions."

As he sat, Gracie asked, "What is their prize anyhow?"

Giving her his best smile, he answered saying, "I don't have one. I have several ideas perhaps, but nothing permanent yet."

"I guess what you need is my help," she asked displaying her sexy smile to him while brushing her hair back on her head as she spoke as if she was ready to work.

As the bell rung for Lunch over, Joey stood looking upon his love saying, "I have an idea that might work but I will have to discuss that with the preacher first?"

Charlie heard the last bit of Mr. Joey's statement and only smiled as he walked by and he could see Mr. Joey had things on his mind and as Mr. Joey attention turn to the children asking him about the contest, Charlie laughed whispering, "or what is in his pants."

But as Gracie exited out onto Hallway Charlie caught her asking, "Or you two married or something?"

All Gracie could say to him being caught off guard was, "Yes, in a way."

Charlie was laughing as he entered Mrs. Shoemaker's Math Class and upon seeing Bill, he said, "I feel Gracie is married or going to be married. I asked and she said, "Yes to both she was and she was going to be?"

Bill just busted out in laughter causing Mrs. Shoemaker to tell him to sit down and be quiet. He did but was filled with laughter more in gladness. He has love Gracie since 1st grade when she was starting to actually live in the world. Always leaving and coming back a crying. Meet a boy saying this is the one and back home saying he was not. She likes the excitement of being a teacher and would always be substituting as she goes to collage to be one. But her wild life was always getting in her way with William's Church getting her to travel with them and sing in some South American church.

Be gone a month or more. He always wanted to go and see what she saw and Gracie wouldn't tell him must about her trips but he did get her tell to him about a trip she had to a Church called, "The Deep Jungle Church" and it was deep in the Jungle too," she said.

She said, "It took them two days to travel by a Bus and she had to sleep in some shaggy motels there and back and while they ended up staying near the church in a tent, they gave the church a great fourteen-day Revival and did the Holy Ghost move for the people. There was healing, many hundreds got baptize and Lord spoke to many through Brother Lewis and she sung good old Gospel songs many she sung in Spanish with some help."

This time Mary Ann pulled an "8" and the extra time of 10 minutes, they had also able to fill the TV screen with a 100 words with a few moments to spare.

All Mr. Joey would tell them it will be a surprise at the end of the Contest. Which Charlie and Bill wondered what it could be and Mary Ann was no help but did retain the idea they were going to win and said so boldly, as they left the room and in the hallway everybody appeared to be in a rush to get home.

Sure enough what was said inside was true for they could see the rolling clouds with thunder in them, coming their way.

Charlie looking at the flashing of lighting asked, "Bill, you'll never make it home. Ride it out at my house then go home and we'll call your house and tell them where you're at. I'm pretty sure you are never going to make it home before it hits us."

"I agree," is all Bill said as they took off peddling fast. Weaving around the cars collecting the children leaving school and down Amherst they flew and were just able to place their bikes in the garage and toward the house they flew just before the downpour came with lots of wind and lighting.

As they ran into the kitchen, Charlie quite winded said, "Wow, that was close. I didn't think we would make it."

"Me either," Bill said still catching his breath.

Mom," Charlie called out leaving Bill who was grabbing a cup to get a drink of water and he hollered "Mom" again as he entered the living room and found her watching the Weatherman on TV describing how the Thunderstorm had form and where it was going.

His Mother gave him her hello smile before saying, "Charlie, before you run up to your room will you fetch me my coffee off the kitchen table?"

As he turned to obey he said, "I'll get it and Bill has taken refuse here and he going call home and tell where he is riding the storm out."

Stopping Charlie asked, "Is that OK with you if he spends the night if it continues to rain if his Mom said it is alright?"

Mom not moving answered saying, "Sure, don't want our Bill to get all wet do we and only if his Mom said "Ok" for after all it is a school night?"

Charlie quickly gathered his Mom's coffee and took it to her telling Bill meet him upstairs and as he entered his room there was Bill setting up his chess board on the floor saying, "Charlie, I think you have beating me the last five games but this time it will be different." Then he shook his head "yes" at Charlie.

Suddenly Gracie open his room's door saying, "What you two doing?"

Her sudden appearance cause both boys to let out a scream before busting out in laughter seeing who it was and she said, "Joey had to move the car to higher ground so we will be spending the night here with you."

Laughter turned to "Oh's" when Joey while spooking his head in saying, "Charlie, why don't you two play on the table out here and see if I can teach you how to play better."

Gracie looked at Joey and began to laugh flashing her engagement ring at Charlie saying, "Look what Joey gave me today. See, I told you I was getting married. Didn't I?"

Charlie stood and instantly left Bill taken a good hold on Gracie's hand and began to look the ring over and is just a small round ring made out of some bright silver looking material and as he let Bill look asked, "It's a silver ring and thought it he give you a diamond ring?"

The words brought Bill and Charlie into laughter as Gracie took back her hand and left their laughter, smiling.

Joey called out from the playroom, "Let's go boys" causing both of them to quickly gather their pieces and the board and on the large stain dark brown table in the playroom before the couch they reset the board and pieces up with Charlie having white.

Gracie came back with soda's saying, "I thought you might be thirsty."

Taking the soda's from Gracie Joey looked into her beautiful face as she reached and kissed him before she left and watching her leave, admired her shapely body and waving long pony tail she flipped back and forth knowing he was watching her when she suddenly turn around and almost at a jump fell into Joey's arms giving him a huge kiss.

Charlie looked over at Joey with Gracie all tied up in him and waited for them to settle down from their kissing to start the game.

Gracie gave Joey a long tongue fighting kiss, removed herself from Joey mouth, Gracie looked at Charlie saying, "Ok, I'll let the game begin."

"Thanks," is all Charlie said looking at his sister with his about time look which only made her laugh quickly joined by all of them which greatly ease the tension that was flowing.

As their laughter settle Joey said, "I'm not going to play the game. I'm here to watch and play it with you for Chess is a game of the mind. I cannot see what you are thinking but I can play along with you and if I see a bad mistake I just laugh thinking I knew you should have move the Knight instead."

Charlie looked at Bill giving him couple eyebrow raises before saying, "Two out of three."

"Oh no," Bill said before sadly saying, "If the rain stops I'll have to go home and hope it floods and I'm stuck here to see what our love birds are doing in the night."

Gracie stood with huff at her brother and Bill before saying, "I'm leaving and let you guys play and I'm going down to help Mother fix supper."

As she enter the kitchen, her Mom was opening one of those large frozen already prepare dinner bags full of chicken and said, "Oops, you caught me how I fix my famous meal chicken meal."

"Yea, right, Mom," Gracie answered as she removed a soda from the fridge but as she stood said, "I can see you are fixing your favorite already fixed chicken meal you liked to fix when you have company."

As she filled the big pot with the bag said, "Why of course I'm fixing it? After all, I don't have a future Son walk into my house without tasting a little of my famous cooking."

Laughter filled the room as she turned on the fire beneath the pot and as she settled herself said, "These flickering lights have me worried our power might go off?"

"At lease you still can cook, you have gas," said as she sat down at the kitchen table.

Mon stirred the pot a second asking, "Gracie, you didn't bring your boyfriend here because he can't park in his parking lot?"

Gracie just laughed saying, "Oh no Mom, that is true but Mother I need to talk to you about our wedding."

Mom looked at her wild daughter asking, "Aren't you moving a little fast about getting married, I mean you just met Joey five days ago?"

"Mom," She returned before saying, "Joey is it and I have found my true love, Mom and, this is no make believe and I'm going marry him in front of the Sixth grade class Saturday after the Contest is over and we already have the Principles OK."

Mom looked at her daughter and could tell there was an excitement in her that has not been there in a while and without thinking said, "Whatever you need me and Dad will see what we can do?"

"Oh thanks Mom," Gracie quickly got up and gave her Mother a big hug saying, "All we need from you and Daddy to get one of those chair lease companies and lease us a hundred chairs for the wedding for the children because we don't have the money to do that being in collage you know?"

Mom said, "I bet Dad and I can swing that for you?"

"If you would that for us it will be great," Gracie answered as she opened the Garlic Butter and as she reached for the Bread asked, "Where's Dad?"

Mon still stirring answered saying, "Since he not here means he stuck at work and over years, you know as well I, he's down in the cellar playing dominoes with Joe, Rex and Frank, drinking beer and will come home drunk."

"That's Dad alright," she said with laughter before asking, "No, really Mom. Where is Daddy?"

"Stuck in traffic," she answered before saying, "He called earlier and said the streets are flooded and he'll be home late and when he gets home he will brag on all about stuff I absolutely I don't need to know about but in a way I do need to know what he did all day."

Gracie laugh saying, "I can understand that. But seriously Mom, there one story about you and Dad that I do not know about is, "How and where did you two first meet?"

"So you want to know how Dad and I met," Mom asked as she sat her rice pot on the stove.

Turned back to Gracie and said, "He did save me and marriage was on the way."

"Then the story is true he saves you from drowning," Gracie asked with raise eye brows added, "Really now Mom, how did he really save you and not one of your made up stories?"

Mom just patted her hand on her heart saying, "He save me from a life of loneliness is what he did."

Gracie seemly frustrated with Mom asked, "Come on and tell me? Then she really asked saying, "Mom?"

Mom turn down the fire under the rice to just a simmer and as she closed the lid said, "I can tell you this, it had nothing to do with a creek and your Dad saving me it was what happen at a carnival one Friday night. I was just out of High School looking for a good man, met some and then your Father and I have been happy, sad, mad, frustrated, angry, hard to put with ever since.

"You have not," Gracie answered before even more frustrated with higher brows saying, "Mom, you going to tell me or not."

Mom stirred the pot before saying, "Alright, if you must know, it was our Lord's doings that put us together."

Now Gracie was thinking one thing and here her Mother goes in another so she asked knowing she going have to dig the story out of her saying, "Now how did the Lord put you two together?

Mom double checked everything before she sat down knowing Gracie wanted her to answered so she answered, "It was a revival by a Tent Preacher name Carlos Leffew and he set it up over at Rainbow Hog where the old race track use to be and people came from far and wide to hear him Preach and Dad and Mom went and I tagged along and met your Dad.

Gracie wanted to laugh as her Mother seem to be thinking back twisting her face back and forth before she said, "I was just out of school looking for a job, a boyfriend and a ride for I had no car. But I didn't know I'll meet the love of my life. He was one of the young handsome young men who had volunteered to help young ladies like me and when our hands touched, he turned to me and asked, "Would you like to go dancing?"

Gracie said, "That was it. That is how you two met?"

"I'm wrong that was not the first time," she answered and while checking the food again said, "It was when our hands touched kneeing before God when it happens."

"What," Gracie asked surprise before laughing saying, "You mean he asked you out while kneeing before God?"

Mom began to do her happy waltz saying, "That he did and God has blessed us ever since."

"But Mom I just love you," Gracie answered.

But Mom stopped her dancing and looked at Gracie asking, "Why don't you make us some garlic toast."

As Mom and Gracie began to talk about what she was going to wear and was Joey her true love and other things and about them, the boys were in an intense battle upstairs with both down to a Queen and a Pawn on the same line with King outside having eating the other pawns.

Joey broke the silence saying, "Looks like a draw to me for whoever attacks is dead meat."

As they were resetting the game Gracie called from the stairs, "Supper's ready."

After the meal, Bill was on the phone begging his Mom to let him spend the night with Charlie does his best begging also.

Joey helped Gracie put the dishes in the dishwasher he turned to Mom saying, "That was the best tasting dish I've had in quite a long time and the garlic toast was the best I think I've ever had."

"Are you trying to flatter me knowing I made the toast," Gracie answered as she left Joey's side and looking into the living room called out, "Charlie, what happen?"

Charlie and shook his head "no" with Bill saying, "Mom said "no" because the rain has stopped and it's a weekday."

Gracie followed them outside saying, "You better be careful going home. You hear me, Bill."

"Yes I will be careful," Bill answered back and as he stated to get on his bike, Bill called toward Gracie from the Garage said, "See you in school tomorrow."

Chapter 12

J OEY SAT LOOKING AT THE SCORES ON BLACK BOARD AND COULD see they were all very close to be even except the first day which so far the kids have not yelled about but he way he saw it, he'll have the last day of the contest be the factor and the only card that has not yet been pulled has been the 4 letter card.

He was thinking as he walked toward the shelves, "I better remove the cards before they enter. Yea, I was thinking of letting the kids decide but since I've added ten minutes to the time all the 6, and 8 letters have been max out on every class that done them but those on the first day."

Then going through the classes cans he pulled the 4 letter card, reshuffled the remaining cards and was just hiding the cards in the desk when suddenly his wondering mind was broken as Gracie stuck her beautiful face in the door saying, "I just saw Principle Jinn and I'm spreading the word that many children parents are calling saying their kid want to be here and there is going to be a lot of absentees today."

She started to leave, stopped, turned back toward Joey asking, "I hope this does not affect the contest?"

"Me too," Joey answered as he was about to stand to walked toward her wanting to give her a good I love you hug and kiss but her smiling face vanish but her thoughts about absentees was unsounded for not one kid was missing on first period as the Wise Girl drew a 24 and he thought the whole class would die right then as a big signed went through it.

Joey gave the class his evil smile saying, "Well, well, the first 24 has been drawn and it happen right here in this class? You have several minutes till the clock reaches 15 so get your words ready?"

Suddenly the Wise Girl stood and looked over the class called out, "We can do this just work as we discuss."

Joey let the clock do the talking and watched how the kids search the dictionary. There was an order in their search from one row to the next. He guessed the Wise Girl had been organizing her team for she was as bossy as he has seen as he watched her sit straight in the chair very aristocratic like, looking like she already has her word ready.

When the bell rung he was surprise there was no rush to the word pad but the Wise Girl and several others but the rest of the class was hunting and only every now and then someone would place a word in and when the class bell rung, there was explosion of "I could not find but two and most I found were already on the board" and there was many "I'm glad that is over."

Joey wanted to laugh as he could see they found twenty-eight words and he was thinking, "I didn't think there was that many in these school dictionaries."

By lunch he was tired of hearing about what happen in the storm and when he sat down at the table beside Gracie said, "Please do not mention anything about the storm last night. The children have informed me enough."

"Me too," Gracie laughed.

After lunch and just before entering Mrs. Shoemakers class Mary Ann had Bill and Charlie cornered saying, "From the scores, we got to and must look good today so I want you two to speed up a little. I've been watching you two slack off toward the end when you could have put two or three words in."

Charlie tried to put up a good fight saying, "All the words I found were taken."

They were actually save by the bell causing her to look seriously at them before huffing and puffing off and all both boys could do was laugh as they followed her and upon catching her Charlie said, "We'll do our best."

"Well you better," she answered back.

As Charlie fell back to Bill, he was laughing and was quickly joined by Bill as enter their Mrs. Shoemaker's math class.

They could see she was reading something and gave them a smile as they quickly found their seats for Charlie had studied thinking pop quiz today but was not sure for she never would give pop tests to any class on Monday but them and she did not do it last week because of the Long Word Contest.

After the bell rung to start the class, Mrs. Shoemaker did not move and motioned for Fred to come pass out her pop quiz saying, "Today is a special day for this class. We are going to have a pop quiz so I can see if you learned anything."

After Fred took the papers from her, Mrs. Shoemaker stood saying, "I know everyone here is concern about Mr. Joey's Long Word Contest but that is English and this is Math and I expect to grade your test results as I always do. You either right or you are wrong."

There were a few laughs from the children at her words.

Still sitting, she watched Fred pass the test papers out and as he laid the excess on her desk to take his seat, Mrs. Shoemaker stood saying, "I hope you had studied the pages in your text book I wanted you to look at and did the homework I told you to do for the rest of the year I'm going to start to introduce you to some higher math, Algebra."

Turning to the blackboard she wrote Algebra with 101 following it and as she returned to her seat she had a smile as she said, "Let me see who knows anything about Algebra and when the bell rings I want you to place the test with your homework on my desk."

But she could see they were already busy answering the twenty-five questions she gave them so she went back to reading her book.

Charlie wanted to laugh as the first question was, "A+B =?" so he wrote "C" down. Many of the questions were of the same kind with missing letters or "If A=6 and C= 10 then what is "B." But it moves into lengths of a triangles and other line formations and by the time the bell rung to end the class, he had answered all the questions and could see Bill and Mary Ann had done the same.

Following the others, he laid his homework and the test on Mrs. Shoemaker's desk, Mary Ann began chanting as she walked out the door, "We are the Six Period Class and are Number 1."

Mrs. Shoemaker just laughed hearing Mary Ann chant her slogan with several others and as May Ann disappeared into the Hallway heading toward her English Class, she could hear many answering her saying that their class was the best.

Charlie and Bill, as they placed their Math book in their locker were laughing as they follow Mary Ann's voice saying, "We can win this contest?"

"I hate to be the one that marries her," Bill said as he closed his locker.

"Yea, "Charlie answered following him, "She'll have me doing this or doing that all my life and all I would want to do is go fishing?"

They were laughing as they enter Mr. Joey's English Class but instantly became quiet as they found their seat examining the board and could see 1st Period had done the 24 letter word with a 28 beside their score.

As the room became quiet, Joey wanted to laugh seeing their concern faces and as the bell rung to start the class, a few stragglers were quickly entering to take their seats.

Smiling, Joey left the desk to say, "Who is going to be the best looking girl in this class today till next period tomorrow?" Betty raised her hand saying, "I will."

Joey smile saying, "Class now we have our good looking and beautiful Betty and I know you will treat her that way tomorrow?"

Pointing at Fred and Frank he smiled saying, "You two pass out the dictionaries and as you can see, we have new ones so try not to damage them please."

Walking to the black board and with a motion of his hand toward it, Joey said, "So far, the record is showing every class to be about even so Mary Ann why don't you pull a card for your letters today?"

Mary Ann quickly left her seat and closing her eyes she reached into the Six Period Can and pulled a card and a sign went through the class for it read 24. Turning to the class she said, "We can beat first Period's count so let's do it."

Joey just watched the children reaction to her words as there was a few "yeas" among them as they began to search the new dictionaries already showing wear from the children's handling.

He was surprise as there were many more children already having a 24 letter word than 1ˢᵗ period to start inputting but that quickly slowed. Most spelled their one word they found right the first time and some did not and when the class bell rung to end their contest they had found the same number of words as 1ˢᵗ Period.

As Charlie and Bill left the class room, Mary Ann was complaining that they should had found more words than the 1ˢᵗ Period Class and it was all their fault.

But Charlie and Bill only laughed at her saying, "Sure it was?"

Joey was writing the 28 on the score line when Gracie entered saying, "Is 28 all the words they found in the dictionary?"

"I'm surprise they found that many," he answered as he turned and gave her a quick kiss on the lips.

Looking at the scores she asked, "How come no one gotten the 4 yet?"

Joey on seeing the class room was empty with a big smile said, "It is for Friday."

"Friday," Gracie asked a little confuse.

Charlie, as he set the caulk on the railing answered saying, "You're the first one to know but Friday I'm having all the classes do four letter words and let the time it takes to fill the screen with words will determined the winner."

"What," she asked surprise before pointing at the blackboard asking, "What about these scores?"

Smiling, Charlie started to turn the equipment off saying, "It is because of the first day scores are hard to enter the game having a shorter time to do so. So to solve this problem, I pulled all the 4 letter cards from their cans and made it the final word basically because it is the only card that has not been pull from their cans."

Watching Joey put a plug in memory chip into the computer to record what had occurred today asked, "When you going to tell them?"

As he finishes, Joey removed the memory chip and turning the system off, answered her with, "I'm been thinking I'll tell them Wednesday. If I do it Thursday be cheating the later classes and the stories they will they will hear that are made up that I'll have to correct."

Gracie led the way out the room, asking, "You still haven't answered me about the scores on the blackboard?"

"I really do not know," Joey answered before adding, "I was thinking of removing all the letters that were done on Monday and that is over half the letters so that want work and I've thought of adding to the word count but I've determine that want work either so I'm just going let them be an experience of finding them and let the four letter word count be the winner of the contest?" He looked seriously at her asking, "What do you think I should do?"

Gracie stopped before entering the hallway and could see Joey had a concern looked on his handsome face and she laugh seeing his predicament before saying, "I think you have the right idea and you must tell them why you did it?"

"Nope," Joey answered before reaching and taking hold of her looking her in the beautiful eyes said, "I think I must act like this was the plan all along my sweetie. If I tell them why I done it will make them mad but so far no one has complained about last Monday so I'm leaving it as if I've plain this all along."

Laughing, she reached and gave him a good tongue rubbing kiss and as they separated said, "It is your funeral so I'm staying out of it."

They were both laughing as he turned the lights out and as they left the room, found only a couple children still running the hallway.

Joey was watching Gracie leave in her car to drive by her Mon's and Dad's, his cell phone rung and seeing on the screen it was his Mom's he was thinking, "How did they find out?" as he said, "Hello Mother."

But her first words were, "Dad and I was wondering how come you didn't tell us you are getting married," and her asked with a little excitement and frustration in her voice.

Joey, thinking how to get out of this without being yell at, said, "Mom, we just decided that yesterday and I've just have not had the time to call you and tell you is all."

"You know we would like to meet her" she asked and before he could have answered she said, "Why don't you bring her over tomorrow after school and show her off to us?"

"I'll do that if Gracie is free," he answered.

"Good," she said before asking, "Do you have the rings?"

"Not yet, but," is all he got out before she continued with, "I did not think so and I know you can't afford them. So we want to know, would you like to have Grandma's and Grandpa's rings?"

Joey was shaking at their words stopping him from opening his car door asking, "I didn't know you had their rings?"

"We don't," she answered, "Word of you getting married has rippled through the family and since Grandpa has died, Grandma called us a couple hours ago and said for me to tell you she wanted you to have your Grandpa's and her rings for your marriage."

News travel fast in his family he was thinking as he said, "Do you want me to go get the rings from her today?"

"Oh know," she answered, "She told us she'll give them to you when you get ready to stand before the preacher."

Joey, as he took a seat in his car said, "Mom, we'll be getting married on the school playground before the six graders this Saturday at noon and they're supposed to be a big barbeque with their parents is our plan?"

"We already know that and we think that is a wonderful idea," she answered before saying, "Bring Gracie by tomorrow and I am not going hear you say, "I can't from you either."

"Yes, mother," he answered as she hung up.

The rings got him to thinking of an engagement ring but "I know is it must be silver looking and I know I can't afford a real one. Shoot I bet Toyshops have just what I need. A ring that is silver. It maybe plastic but I feel their rings I could pay for."

He then looked upward saying, "Thanks for the idea Lord."

Turning on Thirty Fifth St, he calmly parked the car before Barbara's Toys and trying not to seem in a big rush entered and there to meet him was Judy, Susan's friend who had couple years ago tried to get him to date her, but he knew too much about her to do that and he wanted one he had to learn about like Gracie.

"Well, well," she said stopping Charlie but continued saying, "Are you Gracie already having a baby."

Charlie quickly joined her laughter before saying, "I need a good engagement ring and must be silver and" looking on her hands he said, "And the ring must fit your hands."

Judy toke a step back in socked before she gave him a big smile saying, "We have plenty of girl rings that will work Charlie. Even a few gold color ones if you want but I know you are after a good silver ring."

"Thanks right, Judy" he answered and as he walked pass her, Charlie asked "Now where are they?"

Laughing she pointed her answered before she answered saying, "Third row about have way down in the Being Married toy area and there should be some rings there."

Stopping he turn to her, "What's your ring size so I know what size to get Gracie?"

"8," is all she called out to him as he turned to enter the third row. And it was a long row and near the middle of the row as Judy said he came upon the small children's wedding dresses and crowns a whole rack of difference colors rings with most being either gold are silver with most seem to cost around couple dollars.

Joey could see most were plastic but near the bottom was a solid row of bigger rings that were very sliver looking that cost a few dollars more and he smile seeing the rings were metal with a real silver coating calming they would last a life time of love.

Chapter 13

A S JOEY KEPT GLANCING AT THE SILVER RING AS HE DROVE TOWARD his apartment, he could still could see that not all the rain water had drained off for many of the side roads were still filled with water and seeing them, he remembered what Gracie said her Dad told her why he did not get home till almost 12 that night for all the roads were all flooded and the traffic was stuck in it.

His mind wondered back to his love for Gracie then suddenly remembered, "I haven't talked to Brother Harris if he would marry them yet."

Turning on Forty Second, Joey drove hoping he was home. He was his Mon's and Dad's preacher and he known him all his life but since starting collage, he couldn't go to their Church and as he pulled into the Church of God's parking lot and he could see Brother Harris's old truck and car was still there.

"Good, he's home," he thought as he parked his Sprint beside them. Exited and as he walked toward the small house located beside the Church when Brother Harris exited his house wearing his overalls and white t-shirt Joey seen him in all his life.

His almost bald head wore a smile as he said, "Well, well if it not Lonesome's boy who could not visit his old Preacher and the answer your asking is "Sure I'll marry you and your girlfriend Gracie this Saturday at noon."

His words shocked Joey a second before he asked, "I guess God told you I was getting married?"

"Oh no," he answered before almost laughing said, "Your Mother called this morning and asked me if I would."

His answer caused them both to laugh and as Joey settled down he said, "Mother always seemed to know what I'm thinking before I do."

"She told me it was love at first sight," Brother Harris said as he and Joey gave each a good hug.

Letting go, Joey just shook his head back and forth saying, "It seems everybody knows about me but me?"

Again they laughed before Brother Harris said, "Your Mother called me explaining about the wedding and your girlfriend, Gracie had already asked me if I could do your wedding and of course I said, "Yes." Especially with someone I've seen grow up to be such a wonderful man full of God's Holy Spirit."

Joey gave him a smile saying, "I'm sure glad to hear that for I asked our Lord and he said for me just tell Mother and everything be alright and I see it is."

Brother Harris place his hand on Joey's shoulder and very seriously asked, "Why don't we go into the Church out of you know ears and tell me all about this girl name Gracie who has caught your heart."

Joey gave him asides way look and when he did, Brother Harris hand left his shoulder and he began to do his Holy Ghost hop and dance. Gave a shout or two before he seems to be himself as he said, "Sorry Joey I just could not help myself."

His words instantly brought laughter between them and as they entered the Church Joey always thought ever since he was a child it was different as he looked up into hole of the Horn shaped ceiling that Brother Harris had design and built that channel the voices in the Church straight up to God and it worked for when the Spirit would move and worshippers were filled with God's Spirit you could not hear anything outside yet inside the worshippers were doing their worship quite loudly most times.

Joey followed Brother Harris toward his pulpit saying, "Brother Harris, here you are dragging me before the Lord to see if he'll best our marriage."

Brother Harris just motion with his hand while saying, "Not really Joey, I was thinking it was a good quiet talk about what's in store for you once you are married."

But Joey answered almost in a laugh saying, "You don't have to tell me a thing for I think I would like to learn about marriage life as I go if that is alright with you?"

But Brother Harris answered, "Just checking your heart out is all. So tell me all about this girl Gracie."

As they entered out into open area before the Pulpit, Brother Harris took a seat on one of the Church's pews saying, "Father, we have a young man about to be married and as he tells me all about her, will you let him know either to run or stay."

Joey just shook his head and laughed until Brother Harris asked, "Joey, I'm not being funny."

"I do love you Brother Harris," Joey answered before he began to pace the floor saying, "All I can tell you about her is she has a wit about her and she is very smart girl and she catch my eye, then my heart and I'm telling you, I'm in love?"

Walking over to stand head on before the Pulpit he pointed to the ground saying, "A few years ago, right here in this spot I asked the Lord to let me find a girl that would love me as I am and Brother Harris, I've found her and her name is Gracie. She beautiful and charming and she are full of the God's Holy Ghost speaking in tongues. I know God will bless us and our children and Brother Harris, I'm sure I'll be with her till our death. I know she loves me and I love her."

Joey walked back toward Brother Harris asking, "Is there anything else you would like to know about her?"

Brother Harris stood and as he headed for the door said, "You don't have to say anything else Joey for I've heard enough about her from every person that comes to church here been calling me all day wanting to tell me about you and her and wanting to know where you are getting married."

Having to run and catch him, Joey asked, "I thought you were going tell me all your secrets about staying married for fifty years?"

Stopping he turned to Joey saying, "You already know that. It is done in love as you become one and the same for I can tell you that over time you will learn what you can do and what you can't."

Brother Harris was laughing as he left Joey who turned and looking up into the Horn ceiling called out loudly saying, "Thank you Lord for bringing Gracie into my life."

Speaking in tongues he prayed God will bless them as he exited the Church to find Brother Harris was waiting outside and as Joey walked toward him he said, "Supper getting cold so I'll see you Saturday Joey and don't forget the marriage license."

"Yes sir," Joey answered just before he gave Brother Harris a goodbye hug.

As they separated, Brother Harris headed for his house saying, "Supper was ready when you arrived and I hope it isn't cold and remember Joey, do not forget the marriage license?"

Joey watched Brother Harris disappear into the house before getting into his car thinking, "I better get a marriage license that is for sure for knowing Brother Harris, he wants marry us unless I have one."

Then after he had left the Church's parking lot he thought, "This marriage thing is getting out of control. Now I have the whole Church of God's congregation coming to the wedding. Well if they do I hope they bring their barbecue pits?"

Laughing Joey drove home and there in the apartment parking lot was his buddy Rick standing by his old truck fiddling with a fishing pole which he instantly replaced back into his truck bed as he parked.

"Hello Rick," Joey said as he exited his car.

But Rick seemed mad as he answered saying, "I want to know is when were you going to tell me you were getting married and of all things, to a William's Church girl at that?"

Laughing, Joey left his car saying, "I would have called you but Gracie and I just decided yesterday to get married and I bet everybody in town already knows about it? How you find out we were?"

Rick just laughed before he said, "It is hard not too when it is all over town?"

Joey laughed with him before saying, "I guess Mother called you?"

"Not her," he answered before giving Joey a hug saying, "I heard it from Susan who heard it from Judy who heard it from" and both just laughed.

As they settle down, Joey followed Rick to his tail gate and as he let it down for them to sit on he asked, "I sure would like to meet her for she must be something to catch your heart?"

Joey sat down beside him saying, "I've told you already about the Long Word Contest at school with the six graders and I met her there substituting like me and without knowing how, she and I just fell in love and instead of dating forever, we decided to get married this Saturday and I've invited the whole six grade to it and Brother Harris going to be the preacher to marry us and it seems his congregation is coming also and there is supposed to be a barbecue afterward."

"Wow, love at first site," Rick said before asking, "Where are you getting married that will whole all these people and kids?"

Joey laughed before he answered saying, "In the school yard."

Rick laughed with him before asking, "You mean Mr. Jinn is allowing that?" "That what Gracie said," he answered.

Rick stopped his laughing a second saying, "Well you better leave it clean are he will be pissed?"

Joey looked at his friend and laughed with him before saying, "I still have to fine us a marriage license are Brother Harris will not marry us?"

Calmed down, Rick asked, "I wonder if he'll marry Susan and me?"

"I don't know if you want to do that but you can ask him but then Gracie might get mad at me for allowing you into our party," Joey answered.

Rick rubbed his head saying, "I'm not ready for marriage just yet anyway?"

Joey exited the tailgate saying, "If you wait around Gracie should be here anytime now and you can meet her?"

"I can't stay," Rick answered and as he following Joey off the tailgate and as he closed it asked, "I'm going fishing down on the beach and really was wondering would you like to come and fish with me? I already have the bait shrimp."

Joey left him heading for his apartment saying, "I wish I could but not tonight and Rick, why are you going fishing anyway? Isn't the beach water high and rough from the hurricane and I'm glad it's not coming our way?"

As Rick was about to enter his truck, he answered saying, "Best time to go fishing I've heard so I'm going to find out if it is true or not and stop when it gets dark?"

"Good luck," Joey called out as Rick was backing out to leave who called out the window saying, "Wish you were coming?"

Joey watched him leave and as he walked toward his small apartment wondering what he was going to eat, but he was also wondering if Rick was going to catch any fish. They had learned that years ago that putting some bait shrimp in a floating bait bucket, the smell of the shrimp washing in the waves attracted the fish and they could easily catch enough for a good fish fry in no time.

He was drinking a soda watching the news when Gracie came in with two chicken meals from the Deli saying, "I thought I would never get away from Mother?"

Standing to help her and eat he asked, "You did get me their barbeque delight."

"I got it," she answered as she set her food on the kitchen table located in front of the kitchen entrance.

Turning back toward Joey, he took her into his arms saying, "I love you." After they kissed, Gracie said, "You better eat and get your song ready for tonight. You do know at seven you sing?"

As he sat down to eat answered with a smile, "Yes, I do," he answered as she sat down to eat with him.

Later at William's Church Joey position himself under the microforms and began to sing saying,"

He is my very best friend

William Gaillard Ellis, Jr

When I was a child I did not know I just knew that
Jesus save souls
When I grew older I wondered in Sin for Jesus was a
stranger
Yes, Jesus was a stranger till I met him one day and
opened my blinded eyes
Yes Jesus was a stranger I knew him not now he is my
very best friend.

CHORUS:
Yes Jesus was a stranger now he is my friend and gave
me peace assurance
He changed my life, gave me new hope, and became
my very best friend

As I grew older I wonder this world Oh so alone
I fell for all of Satan's tricks until I felt my soul was gone

Then upon my knees one day Jesus entered my lonely
life
Yes, Jesus was a stranger, I knew him not now he is my
very best friend

Now wondering this world gave much joy but I had no
peace within
This stranger was calling, calling me to come out and
be with him
I answered his call though I knew him not now the
Holy Ghost lives within
Yes Jesus was a stranger I knew him not now he is my
very best friend

If you are walking this world all alone and you are
feeling OH SO Blue
This Jesus who's change my life he can change yours too
For Jesus came into this world to bring the love of God
for all
Yes Jesus was a stranger I knew him not now he is my
very best friend

As Joey left the Microphone area, William's Church was worshiping
in tears and as the strength of their tears, filled Joey with God's love and
instantly he got on his knees and began thanking the Lord for Gracie
and the life that God had provided him with having really nothing but
love in it before adding his tongues to his worship.

Gracie broke his worship laying her hand across his back whispered into his ear saying, "Joey, you need to move for the next group of singers."

He wiped the tears as he was helped upped with Gracie's help. He was feeling drunk in the spirit as he moved with Gracie holding onto him, the other group began singing, "There is power, power wonder working power in blood of the Lamb."

Chapter 14

JOEY WAS HAPPY AS HE TURNED ON THE WORD PAD SYSTEM. IT WAS really for no reason but he had this inner spiritual feeling of peace how his life was going when the bossy girl walked in asking, "Mr. Joey, I been wondering why there only one card left in the can when there should be two? I notice there was a card missing when I drew yesterday?"

He looked at her so aristocratic appearance and gave her a smile saying, "You will find out tomorrow and if you would, please do not tell anyone if you can?"

Giving him a big smile, she said, "Way to late, Mr. Joey, way too late? The knowledge of the missing card is already all over the school?"

Joey looked at her realizing what she meant thought, "I guess I better tell them today about the contest change or shall I keep them in wondering?"

But her question did not hurt his spiritual joy as the other children began to enter.

He watched them seat thinking, "I think I'll keep them wondering and tell them as I planned tomorrow. At lease I'll have their attention and as of now, let the rumors fly."

As with other days, the children raced to enter their words and he could see the seriousness in their faces as they tried to spell their word correctly was funny to watch and when the bell rung to end the class as they left some feeling confident they won the word count and some didn't.

He wanted to laugh thinking that two classes had a girl in charge and they seem to be getting the best scores in the game. But Forth period is right there with them with the boy in charge. The other classes don't have any real leader but seem to be doing just about the same as the others.

As he wrote their score on the blackboard in walked in Grandpa's friend he knew as Uncle Bear Ragland saying, "I've been told the operator of the word pad system doesn't really know how to operate it?"

Joey with a surprise look watched Uncle Bear sit down before the computer before he answered saying, "What are you doing Uncle Bear and why are you here?"

As the children began sitting, watching, wondering and whispering, Bear said, "This old baby sure brings back some good memories and it does have a history."

Joey sat back down asking, "Ok Uncle Bear, before you tell me its history, "Why don't you tell me why you are here, please?"

He was hoping the please would work for Uncle Bear Ragland who he has known all his life but Uncle Bear said, "Grandpa called and told me you needed to know how to find the word count and setup a comparison between scored and I can tell you how to do that for I'm the one that program this baby." Joey gave a confuse look asking, "You're the one that programmed her?" "Sure did," he answered before laughing and to Joey, he seemed to be quite happy sitting before the computer key board, seeming to ignore the gathering of children watching him.

As he began calling up the program said, "This word pad system is why I met my other half. It was like a magic union that put us together and I became a good friend to your Grandpa. I was just a young man out of programming school and I was hired to write a program that a person could operate these word pads that was invited by some crazy guy I knew only by the name of Freddy but later, I learn it was the name of a team of crazy Engineers and knowable Science people and they needed programmers to use it with a computer and one of the programmers was the love of my life and of all the programs I've written, this is the only one I will always remember because of her."

But laughing he said, "Just kidding. Your Dad had me reprogram the thing for your class and now with just a few little program settings, you can call up the count of their words at any time you wish and I have this memory card so you can take the data home and just plug it into the computer and analyze away."

As he hit the enter button, he said, "There done." Then after plugging in a memory card in, he looked out into the Class said, "It has always been able to do this but the path to it I did not placed on the screen and old dummy me was thinking, Joey will never need to use it and I can see I was wrong."

Suddenly the bell rung to start the class, he quickly stood saying "Got to go" and as he left the room, waved at the children whispering, "Bye."

Joey did not interrupt his departure with the children and waited until he was gone saying, "Who going to be the handsomest boy in class today?"

The next few classes, as he watched the children fight over finding words, he thought upon just how he could use the power Uncle Bear had giving him using the word count and time.

The more he thought the more he figured the contest still must be won using the four letter Card and he could determine the winner of the other letter groups adjusting each score to first days' time.

As Joey set his food tray beside Gracie saying, "Old Uncle Bear Ragland came by the just before Second Period. He's been Grandpa's friend all my life." "What for," Gracie asked as he gave him a kiss.

Sitting to his food he said, "It seems he had written the program for the Word Pad System. It appears Grandpa got him to come down and fixed the computer screen where I could see the word count at the any running time and I'm not too sure what to do with this new Data. I guess Dad told him I might be needed it?"

Then as he took a bite of his sandwich he thought a second before swallowing saying, "Gracie, I think I'll just continue to do as I plain."

"I think you should," Gracie answered finishing her small lunch of a couple Taco Sticks.

Taking a drink to help wash down a bite, Joey added saying, "But that is not all, the kids know there is a card missing out of their cans."

Laughing, Gracie looked at her Joey and the problem he was in and could not help it but shook her beautiful head and laughed some more before asking, "You still haven't an idea what to give the winning class do you?"

"That I do," Joey quickly answered before taking a good bite of his sandwich.

Still waiting and when Joey continued to eat not saying anything and seeing he wasn't, laughed and frustrated Gracie asked, "I see you not going to tell me are you?"

He gave her his best smile before saying, "I thought you already knew?" "Well I don't," Gracie answered as the bell rung to tell them lunch was over. Standing she gave him a kiss saying, "I love you" and before he could answer her, she exited the lunchroom into the hallway following the students heading for their fifth period class.

Quickly finishing his lunch, Joey followed her into the Hallway when he was confronted with Charlie and Bill and he could see pushing them was Mary Ann watching.

Charlie with Bill's support asked, "There a card missing from the card cans and we were wondering it was the 4 letter card for it is the only one that has not been counted?"

Their question was unsuspected and as he looked upon the want to know faces, he also noticed it also stopped the other children in the hallway to listen to his answer.

Joey gave Charlie and Bill a smile and looking at Mary Ann said, "You want to know why there is a card missing and all I can tell you is wait till tomorrow, I will post the reason on the School's Message Board and in the morning, you can read what I will be doing with the missing number for I will not be answering any questions in class."

He left them not wanting to answer their other questions and as he did Joey boldly in a command voice said, "Understand?"

As Joey left them Mary Ann said, "Come on guys he not going to tell us?" Charlie, watched him leave before turning to Bill saying, "I guess we'll know tomorrow for sure?"

Following Mary Ann, Bill answered in a know it all voice saying "I think he's going test us with it Friday and who has the highest word count wins."

In Mrs. Shoemaker's Math Class, Charlie took his seat and was wondering over the four letter card when Mrs. Shoemaker stood and holding out the test papers boldly said, "I want to congratulate this class as having a perfect score. Not one answered question was missed."

Then setting the paper's down said, "Sometimes I feel I'm wasting my time teaching you math that you will never use. But the main reason math is taught is to give your growing brain a new challenge to face as it grows that you can become an Einstein. That you can build and make objects come to life and mostly to give you an ability to learn to make the right decisions in your life."

She opened her hands toward the children saying, "But when a whole class on a pop quiz make all "A," I have seen a miracle."

Her words and action brought laughter to the class room and as she reached for the test papers Mrs. Shoemaker continued saying, "You must understand you will only live well till your 70 years old. Right now that seems a long off but when you are sixty you will look back and see time flies. So as we dig into algebra will Frank and Judy please pass out yesterday's pop quiz?"

As Frank took the papers from her and upon handing some of the papers to Judy, Mrs. Shoemaker looked at him then to the class saying, "I have signed each thanking you for making my day with a miracle."

Laughter exploded across the room as they looked at the creature image she had stamped by her name and when Charlie got his quiz back there beside her name was the image of a wise looking turtle causing Charlie to quickly join the laughter.

After Mrs. Shoemaker covered more A Plus B Equal C stuff for the class to learn, Charlie stood with the school bell a little fed up with hearing why, how and whatever on Algebra. Placing the quiz paper in the largest text book, Charlie followed and as he entered the hallway, Mary Ann caught him saying, "I can't talk with you after Mr. Joey's class but his girlfriend is your sister. I want you to get her to talk about the missing four letter card and what he's going to do with it then call and tell me what they said?"

As Charlie eyes lit upped, he answered saying, "I'll try" when suddenly he was interrupted, as Charlie hit on the arm saying, "Come on Charlie and quite bugging Mary Ann."

"Me bug her," Charlie said laughing as he gave her a hug saying, "I will try, you have my word on it because I want to know also and I'll call and you call Judy and with her knowing everybody the ball should start rolling then."

Still laughing he left Mary Ann who was in shock thinking, "Charlie did not wine to get out of it but actually going to try to find out?"

She followed them wondering if he could and after Mr. Joey chose the prettiest girl in school, Mary Ann was not crying out "We can do this" she moved slowly wondering about the missing 4 letter card and did it matter anymore about the other letter size words. But stopped her motion when she heard Mr. Joey say, "I know you wondering about the 4 letter word card and I know some of you are thinking the other letters word sizes don't count anymore and believe that the four letter card will determine the winner all I'm going tell you, it will not."

As the room became quiet Mary Ann pulled the 14 letter word card out of the can saying loudly, "We are the sixth period English class and we can win."

Laughter spread through the class as Charlie began digging through the dictionary looking for a fourteen letter word and quickly found a word alcoholisation and when it was his turned quickly place it on the list.

Again and again he found a word that was not used already and had just found wastefulnesses when the bell rung ending the contest causing Charlie to sit back down thinking, "Darn and it was my time to enter a word too."

As Ed and Rex gathered the dictionaries for the class, Mr. Joey said, "Well done and you have the sixteen letter card left to do before facing the doom of the 4 letter card" saying the last bit with his evil sounding voice and a Ha, Ha to go with it before really laughing as the children left the room with some running and laughing as the left.

Joey was turning off the Word Pad System when Gracie entered saying, "Mother called and I got to leave and meet her and the other girls to do several songs tonight at William's Church and they want me to be their lead singer because Bonnie can't be there."

"Lead singer," Joey asked as he wrote 63 on the Sixth Period record line.

Gracie walked to him and giving Joey a kiss said, "I call it that but Mother does not always saying, "Dream on."

Laughing Joey looked at Gracie and her lovely face having her lovely smile on it before he said, "You know I must be there well before seven and when you're going to sing?

"We'll go on at eight and will be singing till ten," Gracie answered before she bent over and gave him another kiss.

Then as Gracie left Joey said, "I must go and pick up Mom and take her over to Frank Ragland's Mansion and determined the songs for me to sing."

Joey stopped her asking, "You're not talking about that big house over on twenty second street?"

"Yes," she answered and as she began to leave again said, "Linda, his wife is the organizer of Mother's group and a great singer. But I have to go, Mother be mad if I don't pick her up in ten minutes."

"Can't wait to hear you sing," he called out to her already missing her lovely body and he was sure she shook her butt at him as she left.

"Darn," Joey said thinking, "I should be thinking of my Lord and here she's got me thinking of her naked behind?"

Joey left the school and as he as he drove into his apartment's parking lot he could see Charlie and Bill sitting beside their bikes, having a windblown hair look and he thought "I bet their seeking info on the 4 letter card?"

As he exited his car, Joey said, "Hi guys, what's brings you?"

Charlie and Bill not moving answered saying, "We just came by to visit before it gets dark."

Joey not stopping said, "If it's just a short visit then let's go inside and get a drink."

Along the way to Joey's apartment, Bill and Charlie began auguring about who was going to ask Joey a question with Charlie giving in as they came to saying, "Ok, I'll do it."

Joey place couple cold drinks on the bar for them and was wondering what they were going to ask. Figuring it was about the 4 letter card?

Grabbing a beer from the fridge Joey asked, "If you have a question asked it?"

Charlie took the two drinks from the counter and as he handed one to Bill, he asked saying, "Mr. Joey, can you tell me about the four letter card and soon as he finished Bill hit him on the shoulder saying, "That is not the question?"

Charlie grabbed Bill and led him away whispering, "If I can get him to answer that question he should answer the other."

Bill stopped him saying, "Ok, ok."

Joey left the kitchen saying to them, "In the morning I will be posting what the end game will be for all to see."

Charlie a little frustrated began to beg with lies saying, "Me and Bill want tell anybody. I promise" with Bill also begging and promising they would be good.

Their enthusiast actions made Joey laugh who said, "Guys, if you want to know you must wait till tomorrow morning and read the post for if I tell you now, it would be unfair to the other kids."

Charlie turned from Joey saying, "Let's go, we are getting nothing out of him."

Bill following said, "Sorry Mr. Joey, we'll wait."

Chapter 15

JOEY OPENED THE CASE HOLDING HIS COLLECTION OF GOSPEL SONGS wondering which song to sing tonight. He had many that he copied from records and tapes that he obtained from the Library or anywhere he could.

Out of the stack of papers he saw the edge of a song he liked to sing when he was lonely and hurt. Pulling the song from the stack and as he looked at it, he laughed thinking, "My childhood writing sure wasn't the best but I wonder could the band play this with me."

Replacing the papers back into his song case he stood thinking, "They just have to follow me."

Leaving the table, he grabbed his old lay around guitar and before positioning the guitar across his chess he places the song on the music stand.

Praying in tongues he continued to thank God thinking, "I use to sing this song all the time especially in tongues when I needed to prayed for some problem I had before me. I still can remember Old Andy, the writer sitting on his porch strumming his guitar singing it when I was out looking for a lawn to mow."

Wanting to laugh as Joey under his breath said, "I remember I copied the song as he song it and gave it the title, "I need your loving touch." I guess that was when I started collecting songs to sing and it must have been God's will for I was just a young boy out having some fun at the time seeking a quarter or two."

Looking over at his stack of songs he remembered, "Yea, he let me mow his yard once a week telling me I could only mow at one o'clock on Saturday and every time I showed up he was singing a different song he had written and I'd copy it as he sung. I did that all summer till one Saturday when I showed he was gone and I never saw him again. I know I got of eight of his gospel songs in there, somewhere."

Putting the music away Joey said, "I guess he died for he was old. I think he was in his nineties. I think he liked to be called Old Andy and there was a wit about him I liked."

Holding his guitar to play laid it down thinking, "I'll never forget the day I met him either. I was pushing my mower down the sidewalk out on Amherst Street looking for a lawn to mow when I came to a large red brick house having a fairly large lounge area surrounded by a short red brick wall with several holes for water to escape when it rains and there sitting in a nice lounge chair was an old man strumming and singing. Seeing his lawn needed mowing I left my mower with my rake and broom hanging off it and listen to him sing when he stopped saying, "Boy, I guess you are looking for a lawn to mow?"

Thinking I already had the job answered saying, "I sure am and I can see your lawn sure needs a good mow job from the best mower in town and that is me and I want to tell you that you sing great and can you play that guitar."

Laughing the old man said, "I'll let you mow for two quarters if you first do me a favor?"

"Sure, what do you want me to do," I answer quickly for I usually only get a quarter.

Still laughing the old man said, "You can call me Old Andy and what do I call you?"

"I'm Joey," I answered.

Old Andy seem real happy as he said, "Well Joey, it nothing real hard. I need someone to make two copies of this song I'm singing. My eyes getting so it is hard for me to see what I'm writing and if you will do that, I'll pay you two quarters for doing that also."

Now I was thinking by now I'll be making a dollar so I said, "I will need paper and pen to do that?"

Seeming real happy, Old Andy said, "Joey, why don't you come up on the porch. I have a pen and paper right here you can use and you can mow afterward."

I settled on a chair and with his paper and pen and I wrote the song down as he sung and he made me take a copy home with me saying, "Now you take a copy home with you and if you come back next Saturday at one o'clock you can mow my lawn for another two quarters and copy another song for me?"

I guess it was through him I really learn about the Lord for he and I would talk after I mowed until his aid, Misses Diane, would tell him the party is over and I must leave.

I still remember his words he said that I will only live well till I'm in my seventies and what was I going to do with my life till then. I could not answer him then and I can't now only that I know I've placed my life in the hands of Jesus and live it.

Suddenly the phone ring which caused him to quickly lay his guitar down and when he answers heard his Mother say, "If you are going eat before you sing tonight you must come by the house and get some of your Dad's barbeque. He said it will be done by the time you get here."

"But Mom," is all Joey got out as his Mother countered with, "There will be none of this I can't come from you. Be here in fifteen minutes."

"Darn," Joey thought as he said, "Yes Mom." "Good," she returned before she hung up.

As Joey exited his car he could smell Dad's smoke from his barbeque pit. The smell made him instantly hungry for he knew his Dad always had great barbeque and Mom always made great potato salad and coleslaw to go with it.

But he also notices a nice Chevy that looked to be made in the 60's parked in the circular driveway he had not seen before which made him wonder who was also here for Dad's barbeque and said to himself, "It's Grandma."

Thinking he'll just grab a bit and run for it was already past six and he had to be there before seven he walked out onto the back porch to be greeted with a hug from his Grandma who said, "About time my favorite grandchild showed up."

Joey smile at her saying, "I can't stay long Grandma. I must be at Williams in thirty minutes to sing."

Grandma gave him another hug which he returned and as she let go she pointed saying, "I want you to meet my new boyfriend."

He follows her point to an old man wearing a long white beard, pony tail under a hat that read "Gone Fishing" who was sitting alone at the patio table.

Leaving him she walked to the table saying, "His name is Ralf Horton and I just love him."

Ralf just gave him a nod as she sat down beside him taken hold of his hand. Grabbing a plate, Joey looked at Ralf wanting to laugh ask, "Do you know what you have gotten yourself into?"

"Not yet," he answered with a low sounding voice, "I just met her Friday."

Joey could not help it and laughed knowing Grandma would bring by a new man for Dad's barbeque almost every week and each time Dad had to do a Barbeque.

As he settled Joey asked, "Where Mom and Dad?"

"Their inside getting dress to hear you sing," Grandma answered with admiration watching him fill his plate with some Barbeque and potato salad.

As he took a seat across from them, Ralf asked, "I'm glad I met you Joey and I've been wondering and I can't get an answer from your parents, so I'm asking you wanting to know is your Grandma dangerous?"

His question caused Joey to laugh again before he said, "You are just being used to get Dad to barbeque. Grandma loves his barbeque and she has learned Dad will fix it if she brings a man by."

"That's not true," Grandma quickly countered before saying, "He does it because he loves me and hopes I'll marry the guy?"

Not wanting get in trouble, Joey as he reached for a forked asked, "That Chevy outside. It looks brand new but it must be thirty years old or more."

Ralf looked at Grandma and answered saying, "That just one of my rides and the 69 Cheval is the one I like to use when driving a good looking women around."

"You have more," Joey asked as he ate and watched Ralf give a smile to Grandma who seemed to blush as he answered saying, "Some people collect stamps. I collect cars."

Joey suddenly realize who Ralf Horton was as he asked, "You own the Car Mausoleum out on Show Boat road leading to Morning Star? There must be a hundred cars in it."

"Me and the Bank do," Ralf answered and as he looked back to Joey said, "Most I do not own but are on display by an owner and there many I sure would like to drive around if I could but do not have the key."

His answer brought a round of laughter and as they settled, Joey finished his Barbeque and as he stood to leave said, "I like you Ralf and Grandma, you got yourself a winner."

As he left the porch, Grandma said, "We'll be there to hear you sing and I want to meet your girlfriend your Mom been telling me about?"

"Sure thing, Grandma and I would love to stay but got to run," he called back hoping he would not be late to do his part in the forty-day worship.

Joey made it with time to spare and positioned the guitar across him as he sat down before the Microphone waiting for the Band to start. He could see Gracie smiling face beside the stage, waiting with the other singers. Her smiling face gave him confidence as he took his eyes off her hearing the worshipers around the stage giving God thanks.

He glace at the song he had chosen as the band suddenly started to play the rhythm he had showed them earlier. Reaching into the Spirit he began singing it saying,

I need your loving touch

Chorus
My Lord, I'm just a child that needs your loving touch
My Lord, I'm just a child that needs your loving touch
I need someone to love me to say it will be alright
Oh God, I need your loving touch
(Repeat several times in worship)

In my Sins I had no hope my life was without a goal
Then a light from heaven came and God's Holy Ghost
filled my soul

You wrote name above and you promise entered my soul
That you will always be in me and will never leave me
out in the cold

There are times I am up and there are times I am down
But your hand of Love has never let me drown
When I'm tempted to stray to follow a path my own way
You always will pick me up and place me on solid ground

As he finished a group of four quickly took his place and he recognized Bobby Berman from high school as one of them who was a great tenor.

Leaving the stage to place his guitar in its case, they began singing a simple worship song of Grace with many in the audience following along and he was met by Charlie and Bill with them saying, "That was great singing, Mr. Joey."

"Thanks," he answered as he adjusting the guitar in its case.

They follow him outside with Charlie asking, "Did you know Gracie was going to be lead singer and can hardly wait to hear her sing."

Joey almost laughing at Charlie's answered, "Yes I know and I can hardly wait to hear her sing myself?"

As he placed his guitar in his car, he laughed with them over Charlie's Mother letting Gracie be the lead singer especially when Charlie said that he remembering that Mother had told Gracie she was too young to be part of their group.

Once inside, Joey and the two boys gain a seat in some empty chairs when Gracie and her Mother's group walked out on the stage. There was cheer from the crowd with many praising God some in tongues. As the other band was leaving the stage, without music to help, the group started to sing "He coming soon."

In several songs Gracie became the leader letting her voice sing out alone for a stanza and Joey could see the group with her lead, sung their hearts out toward the Lord and with thanks. At times Joey felt the Spirit so strong it seems to sing out with them filling him with its presents causing him to sing in tongues with them.

As they sung each song, to Joey they sung with beauty, it seems to lift the Spirit in the place and those gathered rejoice in its presents as

God's Holy Spirit bubbling up and overflowed in the gathering as if Jesus himself had come to listen and Joey notice even Charlie and Bill seem caught up in his presents doing their own Holy Ghost dance as they sung.

Eventually their singing turn ended giving Joey a rest from his worship and as Gracie walked toward him, the Holy Ghost seem to rejoice with him as his heart busted out with love for her loving smiling face, seeming to have the image of joy as she wondered through the crowed of worshipers toward him.

Before he could say anything, Charlie almost at a yell cried out, "Gracie that was great singing."

Bill agreed as well as Joey who gave her a hug which she returned as she met them.

As Joey and her separated Gracie said, "I am bush."

Her words only brought laughter from Charlie and Bill as they in agreeing said, "If I sung for over an hour I would be too."

Their laughter flowed and with praises in back of them as they left for home with Gracie going home with Mom to get a few things. Telling him she'll be spending the night.

Joey entered his apartment thinking of Gracie already feeling alone. She was the first girlfriend he really and truly loved.

Setting his soda on the table he had to laugh as he said, "Yea, I remember Jean in high school and Judy in Jr high but I didn't love them as I do Gracie and right now I must get her off my mind and check this word count data out and see how this is going to work?"

Placing his guitar in its keeping place, he sat down at the computer plugging in the memory card and calling the data up and did Uncle Bear created a program that with a couple key strokes, he could play with the data and there located in the right corner was a special offering and upon see it Joey thought, "Knowing Uncle Bear, that button could get the program wiped out or he could have some sex show and I'm not pushing."

As he began to pull the data, that little button on the computer screen haunting him, gave it one last look saying, "Might as well go away, I'm not pushing."

Looking at the listed number he first thought, "I must make sure words are not been added to their count after the stop time."

When he checks the winners in each word length and was surprise every class had a winner number length saying "I can't think this is possible but the data shows each class has won a word length. But tomorrow may change this but I'll have to see."

Moving into each room count, Joey saw where he could move to each row and determine which row was the fastest in imputing words and who was the fastest overall and of course he had to find the slowest.

Checking farther into Uncle Bear's program, he even found he could even compare each individual's record and Joey quickly ruled that out for they all are winners in his thinking for when it comes to the input, he had notice that if there were kids that could find a word fast and some did it slow and their input speed was reflected in the same nature.

Leaving the computer for bed, Joey had to laugh as he thought, "I guess tomorrow I will prepare for the four letter word contest and I can't use the individual data for I saw in class if a row had three slow imputers and one fast kid or four fast kids and the person who will win each word input would and probably is a lie for the playing field is not equal."

He stopped and thought, "But I could say the same thing about choosing the winning row in each class room or the overall row winner."

While grabbing clean underwear and shirt from the dresser it dawn on him, "To them they are all equal and would never think there is a problem and I could be wrong."

Thought a little more before concluding, "I will use both the row and the individual winner. They want know."

As he stripped preparing for the bathroom, his last thought on the subject before his thoughts moved back to Gracie was, "The four letter card is going to be easy to handle for the Winner takes the crown for the fastest."

Chapter 16

JOEY CAME IN EARLY AND AT THE SCHOOL PRINTER, GOT FOUR copies to hang in the hallway and as he was hanging the last one near the class room, Marybeth came walking by and she seem happy so he asked, "You sure seem happy this morning."

When Joey moved out of the way, she looked at the notice saying, "I am, for I know our class will win."

Joey just laughed shaking his head as he walked into the class room to warm up the equipment.

Maryann stopped at the notice trying to see where their class was ranked. At first it was confusing for there was no winner. Mr. Joey had listed under each letter length, the total word count per room and on each row and listed the top ten individuals. But his words at top caught her attention as she read, "Today and Tomorrow will determine which the best room, the best row in each room, the best word imputer and tomorrow will determine which room is the fastest."

Maryann quickly saw their room had won the eight letter word while 4th period and second 2nd period had won two words but any of the room's rows could be a winner for right now, she could see today and tomorrow will determine the winner with many having close to the same amount of word count.

After several more kids started to gather around studying the notice, she left quickly understanding they needed to win the next two word inputs to win and walking away under her breath she keeps repeating, "We got to win" as she wondered toward the cafeteria for a bit of breakfast for she only had milk and cornflakes before she left home and as she entered, there was Charlie and Bill sitting by themselves waving for her to come sit with them.

"Did you see the notices placed around the hallway," Charlie asked as she sat down eating her sausage and biscuit.

After she swallowed, answered very seriously saying, "Listen guys, its going be rough but we can still win?"

"I don't know if we can," Bill returned quickly

After swallowing she continued with, "I studied the scores and it showed us third right now but I can see today and tomorrow will determine the winner." "But we have the words that have sixteen letters to do," Charlie quickly added.

Maryann looked at their doubt and ignoring their doubtful answers, she counted with, "I know but if we win the next two words, we will have won three words and be declared the winner.

As Maryann boosted up their ego with more "We can win," Joey sat wondering at his desk thinking should he go see if Gracie had arrived.

Ever since he woke up this morning, his mind has been constantly on her, her body, her smile and how she looks at him.

Taking a deep breath, he laughed thinking, "It was the smell of her perfume that did me in and melted my heart, that what did it."

But when the children started coming in talking about his notice, he sat up in the chair and watch them become quiet and he could see there were questions about the notice bubbling around their mouth they wanted to ask.

After they settle down, Joey started the procedure of passing out the dictionaries and choosing the girl to take role count as the kids started to look for their word they needed to fine Joey left his seat and calmly said, "I have answer all your questions in my notices I have placed to the hallway. You will also find your rooms score on it and what you do today and tomorrow will determine the winner so let the game begin."

As he turned to reseat, he catched Gracie taking a peek in. Gave him a smile, looked children and as she left, she moved her mouth such they could see her say without speaking, "Good luck."

Joey quickly left his seat to follow her for he felt his heart she wanted him to take her into his arms and kiss her and in the hallway, she waited and without a kid to see them, she jumped into his arms and they kissed, a good *I love you* kind of kiss and as they parted, she left him saying, "Got to go."

Joey just enter back into the class when a boy name Clifton stood and started to be cheer the kids on to do good and when the clock's neared ten after started calling out loud the last few seconds and when the clock second hand hit twelve he calls out, "Go."

Joey watched the kids scramble to place the word they found on the key board. Some spell theirs wrong and some had to go back for the definition and their attics was quite entertaining allowing him to calm down from meeting Gracie. Some hollering to the one at the seat to hurry and when they spelled the word wrong the frustration they gave was funny.

When Maryann came in at sixth period, Joey was happy the day would be over soon and laughed as she called out, "Let's do this and win?"

Joey repeated what he told all the classes and as they began to enter their word, he watched them do the same as all the classes, miss spell words and forgot the definition but his mind kept wondering back to Gracie and their conversation at lunch about her finding a job and she made the point she wants be staying at Mom and Dad's without him anymore, for she hardly slept a wink thinking of him.

Now Charlie had just entered the word, Undiscriminating, when their time ran out. It was his seventh word input for their just was not a lot of them to find for most of the words were already found by others and that darn dictionary was falling apart making it hard to look through anyway.

He looked at Bill, who just shrugged his shoulders at him while saying. "Hope May Ann happy?"

They both laughed including those around them.

May Ann was bugging Mr. Joey already wanting to know who won and receiving no good answer but "You'll see tomorrow I'm post it" turned to the laughter knowing it was about her and for no reason but joy of being known, she laughed with them and as Charlie and Bill join her she gave them her best smile before saying loudly, "I think we won the 16 letter word."

Bill quickly countered asking, "How do you know we won?"

Not answering, she grabbed her notebooks from off the desk before motioning for them to follow.

Looking at each other Bill motion with his head they better follow. So with notebooks in hand quietly followed her outside and in the Hallway Mary Ann whispered loudly to them with her hand half covering her mouth she saying, "Mr. Joey almost told me so is why."

Charlie looked at Bill and Bill looked at Charlie and together they both busted out in laughter.

Gracie walked out of her room into their laughter and instantly laughed with them as Charlie pointed to Mary Ann saying, "Gracie just told us Mr. Joey told her almost told her we won? I believe her?"

"Well I don't," Bill countered as left them to go home.

"Wait for me," Charlie quickly said and as he adjusted his notebooks and as he followed Bill said, "Bye Gracie."

Gracie did not answer her brother for he wouldn't hear her anyway and as watched she watched him take a few quick steps to be by Bill's side. Auguring about Mary Ann's words with Bill saying, "I don't believe he could know who is the winner just yet is why" with Charlie counting with, "You don't believe we won and I think we did."

Mary Ann suddenly broke her concentration on her bother when she asked her, "Gracie, you do believe me?"

Gracie looked at Mary Ann almost begging for her to believe "They had won" gave Mary Ann her biggest smile as she said, "I do believe you and I guess tomorrow you and I will know for sure?"

Mary Ann quickly said "Thanks," before she turned to run after the boys. She watched Mary Ann's hair stop its waving as she joined the boys and she could see them coward before her causing Gracie to think, "You got them two boys under your thumb for sure. When she says jump, they jump."

She gave herself a small laugh just as Joey exited out into the hallway seeming eager to go home and had this whistle about him as he jumps into the air and kicked his heals causing those that were still at their lockers exploded with laughter.

Joey bowed to them before looking at Gracie, gave her a whistle before saying, "One more day is all that left."

Gracie could not help herself and busted out in laughter seeing the kid in him.

Outside Joey didn't see Gracie's car so he asked her "where" and she said, "At home where it is staying for really it was Mom's car that she never uses so as I was getting the rest of my stuff, Mom took the car back and is why I was running late. I had to get Mom to bring me to school."

Joey looked at Gracie a little confused so he asked, "Why did they do that."

"Dad's fault," she answered.

"Your Dad's fault," Joey asked even now curious than confused.

"It sure is," she replied as she helps out her hand toward Joey gave Joey her sweet smile saying, "It's all Dad fault for telling Mom if we were going to live together, we must learn to share our lives with each other but having two cars is a good way to ruin a good start in a heartbeat."

Her answer was nothing what he expected causing him to burst into laughter and as quickly as he settled, Gracie said, "We need food so I'll drive and drop you off and go shopping. So give me the keys."

Her action surprised him but he could understand her Dad's thinking and as he handed her the keys, gave her a smiled before saying while wanting to laugh, "Your Dad's right, for we must learn to share and learn the lines we cannot cross."

She gave him her meanest look as she quickly answered saying, "I have a few lines you better not cross."

Laughing they entered the car and as Gracie took her seat did not go near the gas pedal remembering hearing Joey say many times, "If I want to start old Betsy I do not touch the gas pedal for I've learned, if I give her gas I'll be hoping she'll start."

On the way home, they talked on what food they needed and especially food that may rot in the fridge and as she pulls into the parking lot they decided go with easy readymade meals thinking it would be best to start with them and let the cupboard grow on its own.

Joey watched Gracie drive off and as she turned out onto the main road, Joey wasted no time entering the apartment inserting the memory disk, press go to open which took a while and by then, he had a beer in one hand as he began to examined the new data and quickly determined nothing had change except now Sixth Period had two wins by winning the sixteen letter word and did it by two words and all the time he analysis that message "push me" would appear and leave.

He would look at the button and it made him wonder just what Uncle Bear had behind that button?

Leaving the button, he calls up the Drafting and Drawing program he uses often for school work.

Choosing a different Award page for each letter length winners with their class period in bold lights and for the four letter word winner he printed all sixth classes as the winner reward preparing.

He wondered if the school will do as he asked and reward the kids with a free meal in the Cafeteria for they were all champs in his view for the Data showed all the word lengths was close with the separation between first place and last place was no more than twenty-five words but the larger words within fifteen words.

Gracie broke his concentration as she entered the apartment carrying four plastic sacks but as he got up to help her, she said, "Sit down."

Placing the bags on the kitchen table, she calmly said, "I want you do know the cooking is my territory and the dishes are yours."

The way she said it was funny to Joey but held his laughter saying, "Sure thing honey as soon as we get some to wash."

Turning to the bags, she gave Joey a glance as she pulled out a burger bag from Jonan's Grill saying, "Now this is what I call cooking my way out of cooking?"

"I agree," Joey answered as left his desk to sit at the table where Gracie was placing couple paper plates, threw the ketchup bags on the table, laid the french-fries on a paper towel and as he took a seat, she pulled two small milkshakes saying, "I hope you like strawberry ?"

"It's my favorite," he quickly answered as he turned the tables heated center on to warm the fries before opening the wrapping around the Burger.

Gracie took a seat opposite saying, "I think Jonan's Grill makes the best smoked burgers for the money anyway, what you been doing?"

After a good taste of his shake, Joey answered speaking with his serious sounding voice said, "I've been getting the awards ready to hand out tomorrow and I think they're great."

"Here, see what you think," Joey said as he stood walked over to the printer adding, "I've made one for each class tomorrow to take but what do you think." Picking up the reward pagers, he set them before Gracie asking, "What do think?"

As she examining the pages, Joey sat back down to finish his meal watching and as she set them on the table looking at Joey with her beautiful smile that had a mischievous look to it asked, "I think they will do great but you haven't got all the rewards."

"I don't," Joey quickly answered instantly thinking, she up to something. Gracie gave him her mischievous smile as she slowly rewrapped her burger asking, "You did say you can check the data for anything didn't you."

"I think I can," Joey retuned and after a pause continued with, "It mostly has to do with the question?"

Gracie handed the award pages back to Joey saying, "I've been thinking we could pick out certain words that we know they will find and the first row to write in the system gets a special awards and a candy bar."

Stopping to take a drink of her shake letting words sink in and Joey did think on her words a second and wanting to burst out in laughter as he answered saying, "We could give them a lot of awards thinking like that."

"No I'm serious," is all Gracie got out breaking up their first argument when her cell phone began play its answer me song, braking eye contact she reached for her phone said, "Dad gave me back my two hundred dollars I had paid Mother for the car."

Joey quickly returned, "I guess you forgot some payments?"

Ignoring his question, Gracie quickly stood saying, "Yes Mother, I'll turn it on."

Quickly walking to the TV control, she flipped the TV on and there was a picture of Joey's class room showing Joey watching the six graders struggle to write their word on the writing pads with the announcer saying, "Yes folks, tomorrow will determine the winner of the craziest contest for children that I've ever seem that their substitute teacher, Joey Williams has come up with to teach children to spell words and tomorrow will be last day of the contest, Mr. Williams called "The Speed Section of the contest."

Motioning toward the children saying, "It's to determine how long it takes to fill one hundred and twenty words having only four letters and that's four letters per child if they can find a word that some other Joker hadn't already put in."

Camera turned back to him as he said, "It has also been reported that the Cable Company right now is setting up cameras in the class room for tomorrow match. The school system has allowed it for the whole community around the school is talking about and everybody wants to watch as well as me, Fred Patch reporting?"

Suddenly it went to the Weather and Gracie frustrated said "Darn" as she flipped to the other channels which were on Weather also so she left it on channel 4 and as she reseated said, "It'll be repeated at 10."

She started to reach for a French-fry and upon feeling the heat on the potatoes pulled her hand back asking, "You mean we have a heated table?"

Slowly, he moved his hands toward the center while saying "See these stains around the center, this was once a Soup table used by the Red Cross when they had to use wood to hold the heaters and to feed thousands and this table got stuck on low so Uncle Lenard found it an action of someone who had been a Red Cross Manager and bought it, got it working again and place a low to high switch and when I move here, gave it to me saying, "Never use high unless a big pot full of goodies sitting on it first."

Calmly he grabbed a few potatoes and as he pulled his hand back, Gracie reached and took a few potatoes while asking, "You mean this is an old Red Cross table to heat big pots of soup."

Joey surmised on her question a second before saying, "That is what I was told."

Gracie looked at the table in a new light admiring the Craftsmen's work as Joey added, "It must have a story behind this table but I don't know it?"

After consuming over half of her burger, Gracie while reaching for a few warm potatoes said, "You would think someone would come knocking after that news report."

"I think I know why they aren't," Joey answered before filling his mouth with a taste of the shake.

Gracie had this got to hear this sound in her voice as she asked, "If you know just tell me why they aren't?"

Joey after he took a sip his milk shake, raise his hand and thumb pointed toward the outside saying, "I just moved here and outside, only our parents, Bill and Sandra know our address. If they're learning anything about me and you I figured both our Moms and Dads right now are showing off our photos and telling them all about us and I'm sure my Mom and Dad is doing that right now."

As their laughter settled Gracie now finish with her food stood saying, "I think I'll go sit on the bed and watched TV, care to join me?"

Chapter 17

As Joey stopped by Big Macs for a sausage and biscuit and as he handed Gracie hers said, "I seems that I cannot get the Natural Geographic show I watch about Locus's after you went to sleep."

"What was it all about," she asked before taking a sip of her coffee.

Taking a big bite of the biscuit and as he drove out on the highway he said, "It was a documentary about Locus's and it showed a locus was once a grasshopper and they seem to be cabalistic and want to eat each other and it said the swarms of locus's is like this, I'm trying to eat the one in front of me and behind me is one trying to eat me so on and so forth."

"That doesn't sound right," she asked after finishing her biscuit.

Joey started to say, "That what they showed."

As he turned into the school parking lot out, on the front steps were several Newsmen and women with camera's auguring with several policemen, who on seeing them, gave them a smile as he pointed and Joey could read his lips which said, "It you want a story there driving in is the teacher you seek now?"

Joey looked at Gracie saying, "This could be fun."

Gracie looked at Joey a second realizing he going to face them so she asked, "Can I tag along and watched?"

"Sure," Joey answered as he parked between a nice looking minivan and an old white truck half loaded with fire wood and as he turned the motor off almost laugh as he looked into Gracie's eye saying, "You wouldn't know it but before taking this sub job, I was thinking of going fishing until Dad asked me did I want their old writing pad system.

That changed my mind about going fishing and after I talked with the Principle, she thought the Sixth grade English class would be the best age for my game and believe me, I had to do a lot of begging to get her to let me set the game up."

Joey glanced into the mirror and on seeing the reporters walking their way, interrupted his story saying, "I guess I better get out and meet them, I got myself into this and nobody can get me out."

Suddenly, as Gracie opened her door she excitedly said, "Not without me you're not."

As she stood, she looked in and with a big smile said, "I want to see what I look like on TV."

Joey could not help it and laughed and was laughing as exited to fine Gracie stopping before the tail gate ready to face the cameras, taking a very sexy stance and was she ever grinning from ear to ear.

A he took a stand beside her, her posture made him take a similar stance ruling out the stand at attention kind of stance, head up, eyes forward and just to be his good old self tapped Gracie lightly saying, "You look pretty now and on TV, I bet you look beautiful."

"Think so," she answered while grabbing hold of his arm she rolled into him whispering "I love you" as she kissed him, first on the cheek and in one thought of love they kissed and Gracie was the aggressor kept sticking her tongue and upon parting her tongue movement told him she like what he did last night."

Watching Gracie reposition beside him he could see she had this image of I hope they got a picture of their kiss and Joey's first thoughts were, "I was just guessing but now I know for sure that Gracie is going to get me in more trouble than I can handle?"

The next surprise came as the only reporter, a quite beautiful dress, women followed by a cameraman came walking up from their right and as Joey prepare for the question, the women went straight to Gracie asking, "Gracie, my name is Dakota Newton and I represent the Singles Network and we at the Network want to know how you two can just meet and in a week get married? We want to know is did you two just fell in Love at first sight or was it something else?"

Shocked at being asked such a question, Gracie stumbled for an answer but Joey saved her saying, "It was not her, it was I that fell in love at first sight and I won her heart easily so we instead of hanging on to our love affair, decided to get married making it permanent."

But the beautiful reporter "There got to be more, was it the sex?"

Gracie put her hand up before Joey to stop as she quietly answers saying, "It was way more than sex for on the very first night, Joey placed his life in me and ask do I want to live it with him and I said I do."

Joey noticing the Children watching said, "Sorry to leave you Dakota but school is calling and we still must face the reporters who are talking to the Principle right now."

Stepping away to let them by and as they left Dakota almost at a shout, cried out, "You two are a good looking couple."

Joey wanted to laugh as took Gracie's hand asking, "Do you think she's talking about us?"

Gracie looked around a second before saying, "I don't see any other couple so it must be us?"

Joey was sure Principle Jinn had been placing the law down on the reporters about not entering the school for they seem humbled as they walked up to stand beside him but Principle Jinn left them with a commanding voice saying, "Don't be long."

Joey quickly stopped her as he asked, "I will need a school Laptop or some other computer this afternoon?"

"I'll bring you one," Principle quickly answered as he left them.

Joey turning to the reporters, quickly held up his hands saying, "I am not going to answer any of your questions, I don't have the time but I can say it has worked out way better than I thought and the consequences of my actions will be presented to the world when I hand out the Awards today at 3:30 in the school's auditorium and the parents are welcome to attend and I guess you are too."

Only one reporter asked a question saying, "Can you predict a winner for us?"

Joey looked at them, not wanting to get questions going decided to answer anyway saying, "I have right now, three class periods standing at first place with each winning two words each and if one of them wins this event today they will be declared the winner or I'll have four winners."

Joey followed Gracie toward the entrance saying, "If you want to know who won, I feel it will the luckiness class that wins today for anyone of them can win."

The children scatter as they left the reporters and after entering the school house, Joey kissed Gracie bye and as he entered his room expecting to see cameras there was none but looking up noticed circling the whole room was a solid row of Cell Phone camera lenses mounted in a white strip almost mating the wall color with several connection union scattered here and there.

His first thought as he walked to his desk was, "Dam, I bet they can focus on anybody with that camera of multiple lenses?"

Glancing back at the cameras, he wanted to laugh as a thought flash in his head, "I know one thing I can't scratch my balls today."

As he turned the system on, Principle Jinn walked in setting a Laptop down on the desk, laid the power plug on top saying, "I want this back after school?" "Yes sir," Joey answered and after the Principle left plugged in the memory card into the Laptop and was checking Uncle Bear's program out to make sure he could use the Laptop when children started to arrive and as he pulled the memory card and plugged it back into the system, he could see they seem very excited and ready to play as the room filled up.

He told one kid to pass out the dictionaries and smiling, he grabbed his coffee cup deciding he needed a cup to start today and found Mrs. Shoemaker, the six grade math teacher filling a large cup and as he walked up she said, "Joey, I think your game has improved every child's thinking for I gave a pop quiz the other day and had two classes where everyone got the questions right and that has never happened as long as I been teaching."

"Thanks Mrs. Shoemaker that is good news to hear," Joey answered as he filled his coffee cup.

"I think it's a miracle myself and the other teachers been saying the same thing about their classes," she added while putting some cream in her cup.

As Joey was left the room, he heard her say after him, "You have great influence over the kids right now so why don't you tell them to prepare to live their life and stay in school."

Joey found the dictionaries were passed out and could see several of the kids searching through it but his thoughts were on Mrs. Shoemaker's words that he had influence over the children which was news to him.

"But what can I tell them," he whispered as took his seat looking out on the class and began to wonder about their future and it hit him, "If I was them, whatever I would say would go in one ear and out the other hoping I would shut up."

As the bell rung to start the class, Joey stood while whispering, "That takes care of talking about their future speech" and looking across the room could nothing but serious faces gave them a smile as he said, "I was going to make a speech but have decided you know the rules. The only difference in this section of the game is how fast as a group you can find one hundred and thirty four letter words? Now are there any questions?"

When none came, he turns toward the table holding the writing pads and pointing toward it said, "I want the game to start different with the first person in the row to sit at the table and enter their word and exactly at ten after, the definition test will show up and start the game. You all have done this hundreds of times so you should be fast at gathering these simple four letter words so better work as a team or the other classes will do it faster so may the best team win."

Joey returned to his seat and watched the two girls and four boys write their word and could see plainly the eagerness to begin the game was written all over their faces.

By the time the sixth grade, everybody was wondering what time they had to beat and as the class bell rung, the first on each row took a seat at the word pad and waited.

Mr. Joey stood and greeting them joylessly saying, "I can see you are ready to roll and I hope you are well organized for you must be to beat the fastest time and its fast. But as I told all the classes you have done this hundreds of times so you could be fast at gathering these simple four letter words so you better work as a team or the other classes will be faster. So write your word on the pad and the game will start when the definition test appears so may the best team wins?"

As with the other classes it didn't take long before repeats stated to appear and by fifteen minutes they came to a standstill for the kids had to start digging for a word and every now and then find a new one.

The only one Joey pay attention to was Charley's as he watched on his second attempt was a repeat word and could see Charley's was getting frustrated as his jinx continued as Joey watch every word he tried was rejected because someone already had entered it.

And as with the other classes, the children gave a great sign of relief as for some unknown reason when Charley inputted "dock" it was accepted ending the game and did he explode with happiness.

As the children settled down Joey stood saying, "The game is over and in a little bit I will make a speech, give out the Awards and answer questions. So first let's see what happens. As I told the other Class Periods, if they could please, sit together if you can but it is not necessary."

Joey they seem excited as he said, "Now go, I need to check the data and should be there in thirty minutes."

Chapter 18

JOEY WALKED OUT ONTO THE AUDITORIUM AND AS HE PLACED THE six large magazines on the table beside the mike stand quickly notice before the stage the sixth graders was sitting on the floor divide into the six class sections clearing the seating for the parents that have showed up and there were many.

He tapped on the mike to see it was alive but before he could say a word someone clapped and in a second the whole auditorium applauded him.

Joey just shook his head saying "yes" across the stands while also saying repeatedly "Thank you."

As the clapping died down, Joey removed the mike and holding it to his mouth began to pace saying, "My name Is Joey Williams I am just a lowly sub- teacher. Now like all of us substitute teachers we usually end up, coming to school for a day and give the kids a test. But this time I had to sub for ten days. Now my Dad had given me their company's old word pad system some months ago and I came up a game I could play with the six graders that would be fun and a learning experience."

Stopping, he replaced the mike in its place saying, "I called the game "Learning Long words."

Opening his briefcase, he looked out into the audience gave them a smile as he said, "I could go into detail about the game but I figure there not a person here doesn't know more about the game then I do and if you really want to know, ask one of the Sixth Graders."

Looking down upon the sixth graders he sharply said, "Isn't that right sixth graders?"

His question instantly got a response from them with most saying, "Yea."

Laughter was their next response with moved into the stands.

Joey waited thinking till it was close to silence before saying, "I want to say first that I've had a great time watching them struggle to fine words. Each word they struggle with always starts fast and does it slow down."

Looking and pointing at the sixth graders continued with, "And you can ask any sixth grader here it's not easy finding twenty-six letter words."

Laughter instantly again spread from sixth graders into the seats behind them.

Joey couldn't help it and laughed with them and as it again became somewhat quiet he took a depth breath before saying, "As I hand out these Awards I want everybody to know to me they are all winners?"

Stepping back from the mike Joey began to clap giving the kids an applause which instantly brought the stands alive with many "Way to go Fred's and Julie's" among the clapping.

The sixth graders just laughed with several standing and taking a bow to the stands and as Joey watch, he could see in the children and their response to the "Way to go's" was nothing but love being a child.

But it quickly ended as Joey said, "I know everybody been wondering which class has won the fastest class."

It was like an instant silence came over the Auditorium which shocked Joey for a second thinking, that was impossible but stood proudly and holding up the Award with a First period as the winner, Joey cried out, "The winner is my First Period class by close to four minutes."

The children in first Period class exploded with joy, laugher and crying, the stands exploded with clapping with many "way to goes" and the other sixth graders booing.

He motions to one of the teachers and handed her the Award, a magazine and a pen saying, "Get first period to sign the back and give the Award to Principle Jinn when their finish. You choose the method for signing."

The clapping quieted as Katy stood herself before the twenty-eight first period's sixth graders and holding the Award up said, "This is your

Award and Mr. Joey wants you to sign the back. But before we begin I want you to sit as you do in class so I the First row to sit here, the second row here, third row here and forth row here."

That got things going after Joey handed the sixth period their Award for winning the eight and sixteenth letter words, he waited for some quiet before saying, "I hate to report there is no absolute winner and we have four first place ties with two wins each."

Rubbing the back of his neck he seemed to deliberate a second before looking over at the first period asking, "I have before me the Worst Class reward and in it I have a true winner. My question to you can I give it? Just a simple "yes or no" for you were not playing for this award. But the winners name will be lost in time but not the one that won the worst Award. But I must warn you that you may have won two words does not mean hilly winks to this reward."

Then pointing at the other classes with a sweep of his arm asked, "What say Yee, but let First Period speak first."

His question seems to confuse them a second before one said, "Yea and quickly the Yea's became one among the classes and waving his hand s for quiet Joey said, "The yea's have and the worst class is Sixth period."

As he handed the Award to the sixth period control teacher he could see Mary Ann blaming Bill and Charlie for them winning the Award and he could see in them was nothing but laughter but there was also a loud sound of relief flowing from the other classes.

Joey did not stop there and continued to hand out Awards to the best Row in each room and proudly called out, "Fourth period second row has one the "Overall Word Getter" Award."

As it became quiet Joey he held more two more Awards saying, "What I have here is special Awards to the class that found my two hidden words. The first word was "fortune" and no other reason than just to see who would be brave enough to enter the second word was "fart" and to my surprise, Fourth Period put it in on their tenth word input and they also won the other Award as the first to enter the word "fortune" before the other classes."

Handing the Awards to teacher for fourth period to sign he turned back to the audience saying, "I'm sorry to say I cannot give an Award to the fastest child for a number of reasons which I want go into."

Seeing he had handed out all the Awards he was going too there a one lone clapper stood and instantly the whole stands and including the children join in giving a great applause.

Joey just gave them a bow seeing a way to escape. Picked up his briefcase and giving Principle Jinn a smile to take over left the stage and the stands only erupted harder in their applause for him.

Gracie was waiting on him and as they stopped at the entrance into the Sixth grade hallway, she said, "Wow, I thought you handle that very professionally."

"Professionally, I was not," Joey answered as he heard Principle Jinn say, "Are there any Sixth Grader would like to say something before we dismiss?"

In the quiet that followed, he heard MaryAnn speak up saying, "I will?"

"Got to hear this," Joey said while motioning Gracie to follow.

But Joey saw she was not alone as Bill and Charlie seem to leading the way or he wasn't sure force and their actions was funny causing the stands and children to have bust of laughter.

Principle Jinn removed the microphone from its holder and before he handed it to her asked, "Are Bill and Charlie going to speak also."

As soon as MaryAnn had the microphone she said, "Oh no, they are my body guards?"

Instantly the whole auditorium erupted in laughter.

Maryann tried to speak several times but Bill and Charlie stood behind her doing fake karate moves and kept the stands laughing until MaryAnn realized what they were doing and with a mean voice, "Please, I'm trying to talk here."

This time she waited until the laughter had died before taking a deep breath watching to make sure Bill or Charlie didn't act up saying, "I want to thank Mr. Joey for providing a different view of words. I have words in me that I will never use and I never would have thought there were so many words that meant the same thing."

Suddenly behind her Bill cried out, "You tell them Maryann?"

She gave Bill a "be quiet" look before continuum with "Before I was interrupted" is all she got out when Charlie cried out, "You tell them Maryann?"

His words brought the audience into instant laughter and right then she decided to ignore them and as it became quiet again with only a few coughs and static talking she said, "If Bill and Charlie will let me speak."

Looking at Charlie she spoke into the mike saying, "I didn't want to be up here alone and thought of getting them to come with me I would give me courage to speak. Now you two, be still?"

Giving them, her "You better or else" look, she turned back to the quiet stands saying, "I want the first say and I think every sixth grader will agree that we never thought school to be this much fun."

Her words instantly brought the whole Sixth Graders class to either burst into laughter with many saying "Yea" followed by the stands.

As it became quiet, she gave Bill and Charlie her evil look before saying, "I remember when I started school I had a great desire to be here but that quickly died off to do I have to be here."

Seeming happy she finished with, "But this contest gave me back this I want to be here attitude that I lost and made me see school in a different light and I want to thank Mr. Joey for letting me find what school really means. Thank you Mr. Joey."

Handing the microphone back to Principle Jinn, Maryann motioned for Bill and Charlie to follow as Principle Jinn asked, "Is there anyone else?"

At his words, Joey left the Auditorium with Gracie following to leave but what Principle Jinn said stopped him with, "If not, before we dismiss I want to say, "I couldn't be more proud of how our community handle this contest for It is obvious the students became very inclusive over it and it is obvious the whole family has also. It is sad to hear we have no class that is the overall winner but it seems we have four classes who are our first place winners with Awards giving to each. I will make a copy of all the Award and sometime next week will present them with a copy for home."

"We better go," Joey said as he could see some parents heading their way and on turning too entered the Hallway they heard Principle Jinn say, "If there is nothing else you are free to leave" followed quickly by the explosion of children's voices.

As they came to his room Joey looked in and seeing the system wasn't there said to Gracie, "I guess Dad had his workers come and get it when school ended and got it while I handed out the Awards?"

But Gracie pushed him inside the room saying, "I think its best we stay in here and wait for while you were out giving Awards, I went searching for our escape and outside the Sixth Grade exit are several reporters waiting for you."

Closing the door, she whispered, "I have the feeling it's either the windows or the reporters and I vote the windows?"

Suddenly Gracie's cells phone began to vibrate and as she answered it heard her Mother say, "Tell Joey, great job and tell him we won't tell anyone where you live or your phone number."

"Thanks Mom, I'll tell him that," she answered and as she heard her Mother hang up suddenly Joey's phone began to buzz.

Joey pulled it from his pants pocket and looking at Gracie open it saying, "Hello."

Quickly a Man's voice returned saying, "Please don't hang up Mr. Williams, I represent the Santa Fe School System and I would like to talk to you about doing the same thing in our school and we'll pay you well for your time."

There was a pause before the voice said, "Can we talk say over a beer at Lugby's Pool Hall over on 6th street at 7 tonight."

Recognizing the voice he quietly answered saying, "Principle Daily, sure I'll meet you and maybe I and you could play a game or two?"

"Good," Principle Daily returned before saying, "Don't tell anyone or we'll have reporters and who knows what coming to question us."

As Joey replaced his cell phone took a deep breath before saying, "Gracie, I can't hide forever and I really don't want too but it appears if they want a story I might as well go out and face the music?"

Opening the door, Joey could see at the far end several children with their parents following were coming their way and motioning Gracie to follow walked toward the exit mostly wondering what was waiting on the other side.

Dear Reader: For me to continue is into another story so I've chosen to end this with a treat. I give you the two winners of the Ugliest Boy and Girl contest.

Ugliest Boy in School

By Charlie

WHEN I WAS BORN, I WAS BORN INTO A FAMILY THAT WAS AT war with the neighbors you might say being that we were the only white folks that choose to live in the roughest part of town. It had something to do Daddy's drinking and Mama's fighting. You see Mama was an Alligator fighter and if she wasn't fighting them she be whipping up on someone around town. I'm sure you heard of her, Alligator Women, the greatest Alligator fighter in the whole world. She works down at the Joe's Alligator Farm on Highway 27.

I was ugly before I was born. Mama had a fight with Crazy Betsey and Betsey had a knife on her and she stabbed Mama in the belly and I was inside Mama and was stabbed also. It made me look like this ugly creature you see with its hunched back and all. Mama tells me I'm going to be famous after I told her about some movie director wanting to put me in his movie. It has something to do with me being so ugly.

In school, for a time I was not happy. I was called ugly, humped back Kid and many more names especially if I mess up in a game we were playing.

Sometimes I wanted to smash their face in but Mama told me to take the insults because they were right, "I was the ugliest boy in school."

It got so I was even making up a few names for myself like "Ugly and handsome" and my best was "Ugly Crazy" and one time I went home and Mama heard me say, "Ugly Crazy is home." All hell broke loose and Mama fussed on me for calling myself Ugly with a Crazy to go with it and went on and on about loving myself and love others and

I'm thinking why was Mama talking that way, for to know Mama, she would rather give a black eye then a hand shake. I even heard Daddy say, "When you see Mama walking down the road you best run especially if she wearing her war paints."

Now in school, I was always being used to scare the new kid in class. Ever since kindergarten, Carl and Paul would hide me and when the girl or boy came to answer their calling, I would jump out and say "Hi." It usually made them give a little scream when I did and that was when I learn girls can hurt for most of the time I ended up with a black eye for scaring them and that black eye only made me uglier. Still it was funny to watch their reaction upon seeing me.

Another thing I liked to do was go on School trips for on them I get to see the world around and meet so many people and I liked to see their reactions upon seeing ugly me. The last school trip was when we had that last Earthquake. This trip we went to Hero's Playland Park and the Earthquake broke the foundation of the Fairest Wheel. Bobby my friend was riding it and was knock out of his seat like some others and like Bobby, was left hanging and screaming "Someone help me." I really don't know what happen I just reacted and quickly using my hunchback abilities, I climbed up onto that Fairest Wheel saving Bobby and six others.

Mother told me that is when my true self showed itself for by knowing how ugly I was. She said words and insults mean nothing because I am an ugly 12-year-old boy so I should not be ashamed for showing off and use my Hunchback abilities and save my friend."

Well must go I hear Mama calling and I hope some of you Reporters are still here when I come back. I'm leaving for a meeting with my director today and he is going to show me," then he hunches his back showing his ugliness and discussing self before continuing with, "the ugliest kid in school, I am about to become famous. Bye now."

The ugliest girl in school

By MaryAnn

As I hobbled into the kitchen letting the screen door behind me, I said, "Mother, I was happy when I walked up to Mr. Joey to obtain the ugliest girl in the sixth grade award."

"When they start giving out Awards for being ugly," Mama asked as she turned from the sink drying her hands.

As I slide myself into my favorite chair at the kitchen table answered saying, "It was Mr. Joey's idea and I won it."

Mama watching me sit she added, "So you won the ugliest Girl Award. Why don't you tell me all about it?"

"It started yesterday," I quickly answer eyeing the apple on the table, fighting the ergs to eat it before saying, "Yesterday, Mr. Joey had us enter a name on a computer who we thought was the ugliest and when a name was enter ten times it was listed on the voting screen and ugly Francis Big Butt thought she was going to win but I won by a landslide."

Mama was laughing as she placed a glass of tea and cookie before me saying, "To them your ugly but to me you're my sweet thing and how ugly you are makes me no different."

"Aah Mama," I answered and as I picked the cookie upped and I very frustrated said, "You don't understand, Mama. I proud to be the ugliest girl in school, it was Charlie and Bill and some other boys were calling me the prettiest girl instead of the ugliest girl and I wanted to whip up on all of them."

Mama wanted to laugh as she said, "I have to admit you are ugly and I can see those boys had no right for calling you beautiful and knowing how ugly you are I think it would make me mad also."

Not sure how to tell Mama so I decided just to confess, took a deep breath before saying, "Mama, mad really is not the word to use. As I was walking by Charlie's desk he said, "Hey, beautiful" and I just went crazy and hit him and left the class room just a crying."

"Wow, you sure were mad at Charlie," Mama asked watching me consume what was left of my cookie.

Looking up at Mama I gave her a smile saying, "I wasn't mad at Charlie for him calling me beautiful Mama. I was angry because Charlie saw beauty in me I did not think I had any and I sure didn't want to be call beautiful for sure. I like being ugly."

As Mon set another cookie before me she laughs as she said, "I've been telling you what would happen if you took a bath, comb your hair, put on clean clothes what will happen?"

"I had too," I replied.

"Why," Mom asked returning to the sink.

"I smelled so bad even the dog wouldn't get near me is why," I answered as I consume the cookie looking for another.

"That bad," Mom asked.

"I sure was," I return wondering will I get another cookie before saying, "At school when I walk down the hall the other kids were gagging and holding their noses and I knew I must need a bath. I don't mind being ugly but smelling I don't like."

"You know it comes with being an ugly girl," Mom returned.

Standing, I open my arms saying, "Mom, just look at me. I must wear a pair of Dad's shoes my feet are so big, I have a knock knee walk, my butt is so big I must sit on two toilet seat to pee, I can't wear a brassier for I have no tits yet, buck teeth, very large nose, three eye brows over one brown eye and only one eye brow over my blue eye, hair that want stay combed and sticks out everywhere, one arm shorter than the other with one hand way larger than the other and what really makes me ugly my skin is white, brown, black and blue and my hairy ears are large and rounded and stick out facing forward and I weight over three hundred pounds."

As I took a seat back at the table, Mom just smile as she said, "That may be what you look like but your still my sweet little baby."

"Aah Mom," I returned.

Printed in the United States
by Baker & Taylor Publisher Services